THE
HUNGRY
GENERATIONS

THE
HUNGRY
GENERATIONS

DAVID
GILMOUR

SINCLAIR-STEVENSON LTD

First published in Great Britain by
Sinclair-Stevenson Limited
7/8 Kendrick Mews
London SW7 3HG, England

Copyright © 1991 by David Gilmour

British Library Cataloguing in Publication Data
A CIP catalogue record for this book is available from the British Library.

ISBN: 1 85619 069 2

Typeset by Rowland Phototypesetting Limited
Bury St Edmunds, Suffolk
Printed and bound in Great Britain by
Billing & Sons Ltd, Worcester

To Sarah

And if you are wise
you will never pity the past
for what it did not know,
but pity yourself for what
it did.

John Fowles, *The Magus*

THE
HUNGRY
GENERATIONS

Chapter One

The library hearth had always seemed the strategic centre of the house at Starne. Whoever stood there, with his back to the great marble fireplace, appeared to establish a dominance, almost a moral ascendancy, over his seated listeners. It was my grandfather's favourite position. I remember him standing there after dinner, leaning against the mantelpiece in his green velvet jacket as he expounded the glories of West Indian cricket. And I recall him in the same place in more sombre temper, preparing for a quarrel with the factor. While he awaited the man's arrival, he tapped ominously with his riding whip the calf of one boot. He was in so volcanic a rage I feared he was going to flay poor Mr Logan.

I used to imagine important visitors standing before the library fireplace in declamatory mood, throwing off remarks that would be repeated within the family for years afterwards. General Haig had stood there, I know, warning my grandfather after the Great War that Britain must never again rely upon the French. 'They've been bled white, Archie, they'll take generations to recover.' Many years later Churchill had stayed and spent an evening denouncing Chamberlain. And Chamberlain himself had come, exhausted after Munich, but no one had remembered what he said. I don't know if my father met Kipling at Starne or in London, but in my imagination their confrontation had taken place in the library. 'I hate your generation,' the old man had said bitterly, 'I hate you because you are going to give it all away.' Had Kipling lived to see the Suez crisis, he would have hated my father still more.

But today, I realized, everything was wrong, everything a travesty of accumulated tradition. Even the fireplace was wrong. In my grandfather's time sweet-smelling birch logs blazed in a fire that was never extinguished between the beginning of autumn and the end of spring. But today there was no blaze, only the acrid smoke of an elm branch cut from a diseased giant which had fallen in the last autumn gales.

Everything had irritated me that morning: the comments of the accountant, the report of the estate agent, Logan's eager expressions of agreement with each new suggestion. Various schemes had been put forward, each worse than the last: to divide the house into flats, to convert it to an hotel, to develop it as a country club. But nothing irritated me more than the behaviour of the lawyer, who was standing in my grandfather's place by the fire and summing up with pedantic primness the advantages and drawbacks of each proposal.

'If I may repeat myself,' he was saying, 'we should never forget what we are aiming for. To generate sufficient funds to meet the tax liabilities consequent upon your father's death. And to establish the family, once and for all, on a firm financial basis.'

He looked at me over the top of his spectacles as if to ascertain whether I needed a third explanation of something so obvious.

'With all respect,' he went on, 'to your father and grandfather, neither of their lordships were thrifty men. Your grandfather, in particular, spent a not inconsiderable sum of money, and when he required more, he looked around for something else to sell.'

I disliked this man and was tempted to tell him I thought it a reasonable way of surviving. I was glad that my grandfather had not been one of those Scottish lairds who were proud of their meanness, who kept cashbooks for tram fares and church collections, who installed coin-operated telephones in the guest bedrooms.

'I think I can safely say,' the lawyer was reiterating, 'that we have reviewed all the options. There can be little doubt, I fear, that the sale of the house and some of its contents should go ahead. Our one remaining task is to decide which is the best way of maximizing the proceeds.'

Once again he tucked his chin into his chest and his presbyterian blue eyes stared at me over the steel rims. He evidently felt he had completed his duty, both moral and professional, and that an opinion was now required from me. But at that moment Mrs Ross the housekeeper entered with a trolley of beer and sandwiches, and I was spared the need to answer.

'Gentlemen,' I said after handing around the drinks. 'I need some time to think about this. Shall we adjourn for an hour?'

I left them with relief, oppressed by feelings of indecision and resentment. I had arrived that morning on the night sleeper from London and already they were expecting answers. Of course they had been sending me suggestions and ideas since my father's death some months before, and doubtless they felt I had been given enough time to make up my mind. But none of their proposals had tempted me. Every letter had merely made it clearer that they had no sympathy with my dilemma or even realized that a dilemma existed. They assumed I could view the sale of my home, the house which had belonged to my family for over three centuries, as a simple business deal.

I walked along the library passage, across the inner hall and up the great oak staircase. On the landing I stopped, as I used to do as a child, and looked at myself reflected a dozen times in opposing wall mirrors. I had once been proud of my reddish colouring, which I used to ascribe to our Celtic ancestors. But I was darker now, as well as taller, and my King's Road clothes and shoulder-length hair would have gone uncomfortably with the portraits of bewigged forebears. These were hung in the gallery above the inner hall and arranged in chronological order. I went around the balustraded passage against the years and so came first to my grandfather, painted in his burberry as he leant against a stone wall. Beyond him were his father, an uncle who had killed himself accidentally when cleaning a shotgun, and a group of whiskered Victorians. The portraits were badly labelled but I had heard my grandmother describing them so often to visitors that I could not forget who they were. There was the admiral and his wife, painted by Lawrence, there the governor-general of Canada, there the second earl who had been such an earnest agricultural reformer in the Lothians. He knew all about Trencher ploughs and the rotation of crops; he understood which eyes of a potato should be cut and which left for sprouting. Regarding that clean-shaven face, possessing all the assurance of the Enlightenment, I flinched at the thought of what I was meant to do.

My favourite pictures were of less successful relations. One portrayed a young man with a lute dressed in a velvet suit and a fur-lined coat; he had pale handsome features and had died early of consumption. The other was a portrait of the arrogant Lord Kenmure, beheaded for treason after the first Jacobite rebellion. I know now that

4

he was more or less a bandit who used a barrel of brandy as his standard and looted the south-west, but as a child I had thought of him as a hero who stayed loyal to the Stuarts when the rest of Galloway had betrayed them. He died well on the scaffold, jesting that he had not bothered to buy a suit of mourning because he expected a reprieve. In the muniment room we kept a macabre collection of his last possessions, the night cap he had worn during those final hours, the execution warrant, 'the Grand Indictment of High Treason exhibited against' him. In his bible the last lesson he had read to himself was marked with a K in his own blood.

From the gallery a long passage panelled in dark oak ran past the guest bedrooms to the nursery wing. On the walls hung the favourite pictures of my childhood, Flemish battle scenes of the seventeenth and eighteenth centuries. The last one on the left had long held a morbid fascination for me – the fascination of so many tales of Scottish history which combined valour with horror and treachery. It showed a fine cavalier, plumed and breast-plated on a white horse, at the moment of receiving a mortal wound in the back from a repellent murky figure with a musket.

It was a long time since I had been to the nursery wing. I had not lived at Starne for a dozen years and in recent times had come only for short visits, to be with my father in his solitude and his last illness. My life and my future had been in London, and Starne had seemed to belong to a past I wished neither to explore nor to resurrect. Yet now that I was confronted by its imminent disappearance, it seemed necessary at least to investigate. So I went to the end of that passage for the first time in a decade, eager but nervous, conscious that I would encounter the ghosts of my childhood, among them my nanny, my young brother, even, although she was still alive, my mother.

I did not know if I wanted to find it changed or unchanged, cared for or abandoned, but in the end I was glad that the nursery wing was clean and largely unaltered. The pictures were still there, prints of the Border hunts, a pair of watercolours of wild geese at dawn. So was the rocking-horse, though it seemed more battered than I remembered; it had lost a stirrup and most of its mane and tail. Some fox brushes, collected by my cousins one winter, had hung from a brass hook in the wall, but these fortunately had been removed. The bathroom too was little changed: no one had put away the old tin tray with its faded picture of a mountain and a Swiss lake. It had always been on top of the low medicine cupboard bearing a group of permanent residents – bottles of Minadex, Lucozade and the blue milk of magnesia – as well as temporary lodgers like cough mixture and throat pastilles.

The door of the day nursery seemed locked and I felt a moment's relief that I would not have to enter. But the handle was only stiff and I soon found myself in front of the familiar screen with its collage of pictures cut out of Edwardian magazines. The room, once the centre of my existence, seemed to have shrunk; even the great sofa, whose arms we had used as cavalry horses, was now of ordinary dimensions. Here again little had changed: my childhood books were still in the bookcase, the miniature chairs with wicker backs were still grouped in their corner, the rocking boat and other wooden toys made for us by an estate joiner still occupied their old positions. The ornaments had been taken off their shelves, presumably to make the dusting easier, but in a drawer I found the gifts my parents had brought back from their foreign travels: a straw camel, a plastic gondola, a beautifully carved leopard from Kenya.

Opening the toy cupboard brought back memories I would have preferred to forget. I could remember little about my brother, who was two years younger than me and died at the age of five, and my picture of him now is formed from the photographs in my grandmother's album. Yet I could still remember which were his toys and which were mine, which farm animals he had been given and which had come to me. I pulled out his old farmyard and some of the animals: they represented a Britain which had not existed even when they were new, a land of duck ponds and carthorses, of farmers on horseback and geese in the yard. Another anachronism was my 'Victory' jigsaw puzzle of Scotland. Over the years it had lost some of its counties, but I could remember them well. They had helped to form my idea of Scotland, those little pieces with the black cows in Angus, the sheep and whisky in Argyllshire, the ships of Renfrew and the coal mines of Lanark. And farther north, beyond the Highland cattle, were the great stags, the fish of Sutherland, and a kilted man tossing the caber.

The nurseries were linked to the ground floor by a stone staircase inside a turret. Its winding steps wept with the onset of rain, the light sandstone turning an ominous grey. But they were pale that day for the weather was fine and the snow was disappearing, leaving only thin lines of white behind the hedges and on the north sides of the garden walls. I looked through a window of the turret at the dappled landscape of garden and park, all in shades of dun and winter green, and beyond them to the contours of woods and fields which descended gradually to the coast. The day was so clear I could see the tankers in the Forth and the fishing villages of Fife.

The crack of billiard balls could be heard as I reached the garden corridor, and I went to see who was about.

My great-uncle Fitzroy was playing by himself on a worn and badly-scratched cloth.

'Ah, there you are,' he said, straightening. 'They told me you were coming up.'

'Yes, I arrived this morning. How are you?'

'Tolerably well, dear boy. Not getting any younger, of course, but tolerably well all the same.'

He beamed at me good-humouredly, fingering his thick grey moustache. He was a large awkward man, my grandfather's youngest brother, and a genial and reassuring presence throughout my childhood. When I was young he had asked me what Santa Claus had brought for Christmas; and when I was older he used to ask what I intended doing when I grew up. Perhaps realizing that both questions were now redundant and unable to think of anything else to say, he leant forward once more with his billiard cue. The shot was successful but the pockets were so full of holes that the ball landed on the floor.

'Met some extraordinary fellows in the library,' he said, rubbing chalk on the end of his cue. 'Drinking beer.'

'Yes, I invited them.'

'Friends of yours?' he asked, his eyebrows indicating surprise.

'No, not exactly. Logan was there with Reid and Fletcher the lawyer. Do you remember Fletcher?'

Uncle Fitzroy frowned in concentration. 'I think I knew his father.'

'We were discussing the sale of the house.'

'Ah yes, dear me, a sad business.'

There was another pause. Uncle Fitzroy had lived at Starne longer than anyone. Retiring from the navy at the end of the Second World War, he had returned to the house and stayed there ever since. He did not marry and never left the estate except for an occasional day's shooting and a monthly visit to the New Club in Edinburgh. The unalterable fixture of his routine at Starne was winding the clocks and checking the barometer.

'I hear you are going to North Berwick,' I said.

He bowed slightly. 'Your Aunt Pamela has been good enough to find me a room in some establishment. But I shall enjoy it,' he added cheerfully. 'I'm still good for a few years of walks by the sea and the odd round of golf.'

'I hope you'll be happy there.'

'I'm sure I will. Still,' he remarked, gesturing vaguely at the billiard table and the rest of the room, 'it seems a pity to lose all this. Don't know much about dates and history and all that, but we've been here an uncommonly long time – in fact we built the place – and it sort of doesn't seem right for other people – I mean Americans and Japanese and whatnot – to be here instead of us. Do you see what I'm driving at?'

'Yes, of course. I'm upset about it too.'

He took his watch from his waistcoat pocket and studied it. I remembered how he used to call it his timepiece and tell us children to blow hard so that it would open. He continued to do this long after we had understood how the mechanism worked.

'Time for a little something,' he announced with a fresh smile.

That was also reminiscent of childhood, a remark he always made when he was thirsty and one which inevitably associated him with the comforting figure of Winnie the Pooh. In Uncle Fitzroy's case the 'something' was not of course honey but vodka, or 'vodders' as he called it. I remembered how he had once instructed me to prepare 'vodders on the rocks' by pouring the spirit on to the ice rather than dropping the cubes into the vodka. It was very important, he assured me, but he never explained why.

My uncle ambled towards his rooms and I sat on a

radiator by the window, looking to the south this time, at the long low lines of the Lammermuir hills and the sun which even in the early February afternoon seemed unnaturally close to the horizon. The house was quiet and desolate. It needed people, a large family and many guests, and now there were only Fitzroy and myself, apart from an aunt and some cousins who occasionally visited. We had never bred much and there had been a tragedy in every generation: a great-uncle on the Somme, my father's elder brother in North Africa, my own small brother in a burn in those hills, drowned after stunning himself in twelve inches of water.

Yet even with tragedy the house had been alive. There had been guests and servants, housemaids cleaning the rooms, the butler cleaning the silver, my grandmother's maid arranging the flowers in the red drawing room. There was always laughter in the scullery or the servants' hall or the brushing room where a Croatian valet polished my grandfather's shoes so that they gleamed like conkers. And laughter surrounded my grandmother, who insisted on being with people who talked well and amused her. I recalled the young men who charmed and flattered her, men who were witty and effete and mildly malicious, who talked constantly in exaggerated accents with unfamiliar stresses about paintings and architecture and their acquaintances. But there had been no amusing people in the house for a long time; perhaps no one had made a joke there for a dozen years.

The gardens had been similarly depopulated. A photograph in the cloakroom showed the head gardener in 1885 with his staff of twenty-five. Now there was a single gardener with a boy and a pensioner who cycled in from the village on three mornings a week. The formal beds had been grassed over in my grandparents' day, though you could still make out the geometrical patterns from the top windows of the house. Four full-time gardeners had been employed and castigated by my grandmother. 'Four gardeners,' she used to exclaim, 'and they can't produce a decent lettuce between them!'

There was no one in the garden when I went out, no one in the orchard or the remaining herbaceous border, no one in the high hot-houses among the massive rusty pipes. Yet once the garden had been a peopled place: my mother used to complain that she could never read for ten minutes in a deckchair without being approached by someone. She had a special aversion to my friend the mole-catcher who turned up at unexpected times to study the runs and position his traps. I remember him looking at the molehills and feeling the ground with his feet, pressing slightly, and then finding the runs fifty yards away. That man with his ruddy face and pale blue eyes taught me much about the ways of animals. I remember him bending down and showing me a young poplar with a lacerated bark, 'That's been done by a roebuck, right enough. Marking his territory with his horns.'

Yet though my old friends were not there, the garden retained some secrets and traditions. I recognized the stems of the Malmaison rose brought from Nice a century ago, and close by the myrtle used in my aunt's wedding bouquet. Beyond the walled garden was the lily pond with a sunken punt, and then the place my grandmother had chosen as a cemetery for her dogs; marble worktops had been sawn up and used as headstones to commemorate a succession of golden labradors. Farther on stood the summer house and the ancient yew I had used as a tree camp. I thought of going to see if anything remained of the thatch and the nailed planks, but I did not. I had encountered enough remnants of my early life that day.

I went instead through the orchard and down to the burn. Both banks were carpeted with early snowdrops which in April would give way to wild garlic. From the bridge the great beech avenue began, the trees pruned high up on the trunk, their branches spreading across the path and interlocking forty feet above me so that they gave the impression of forming a gothic nave. Beyond stood a single giant tree which like the others still stubbornly retained last year's leaves, but it had never been pruned and now it seemed twisted and deformed, its pale branches hanging down like vast elephant trunks.

On my way back to the house I came across the gardener, a short wiry man with a soft voice and a slow smile. His name was Brown but everyone except my family called him Hovis, or usually Wee Hovis to distinguish him from his slightly taller brother.

'I heard you were coming up.'

'Just a short visit, I'm afraid.'

'Aye, that's what I'm told.' He added, 'It's a grand day for your visit though.'

'What have you been told?' I asked sharply.

The gentle smile broke over his face.

'That it's a sad day for the Gordons of Starne and there'll be big changes hereabouts.'

We both looked towards the great south front of the house. No one could have claimed it was a beautiful building, for the classical unity had been destroyed by too many additions in the last century. Yet never had it seemed so appealing as on that still, melancholy afternoon; and never since my childhood had I experienced such a strong feeling of possessiveness.

'I don't yet know,' I said slowly, 'what changes there'll be. Places like this shouldn't have to change.'

It was well over an hour since I had left the library, but I did not want to return yet. I made my way to the study and sat down behind the heavy mahogany desk of my father and grandfather. I pulled open a few drawers, fiddled idly with a box of spare nibs, looked up at the shelves of leather-bound books. The room smelt as always of that musty combination of leather and pipe tobacco even though it was several months since a pipe had been smoked there. But then every room retained its distinctive smell. There were no longer lilies or Turkish cigarettes in the red drawing room, but I could have gone there with my eyes shut and known where I was from the smell. And it would have been the same with the other rooms: the cloakroom with its smell of mothballs and old burberries, the garden room with its tang of discarded daffodil stalks. Every room had a sensual character of its own; I could have identified them from the ticking of their clocks.

During my years in London I had never managed to forget Scotland or my upbringing at Starne. It was true that I regarded my childhood as privileged and feudal, a past to be ashamed of and in need of expiation. And certainly I thought the work I did with my wife in London was useful and, as we used to say, 'relevant'. Grouse moors and Scottish reels were decadent, obsolete, abhorrent. Real life was working for the causes of the Third World, the committees for the freedom of this or that, the charitable trusts for the victims of authoritarian dictatorships. Yet I was always aware, as I sat among the pamphlets and plastic coffee cups of those interminable meetings, that my ties to Starne were immanent and inalienable.

In London I unconsciously retained a rural calendar. I found myself looking at the day and thinking, 'now I used to help with the haymaking' or 'now is the time for bringing out my skating boots'. One November morning I looked up past the grey Earls Court flats and thought, 'the geese will be flying south now'. This nostalgia and sentimentalism discomforted. Why did indifferent verses from Scottish poets come back to me again and again when I could seldom remember the works of English writers? Scott's lines in particular seemed to mock and subvert everything I was trying to achieve:

> Land of my sires! what mortal hand
> Can e'er untie the filial band
> That knits me to thy rugged strand?

One afternoon I passed a Scots fiddler in an underground station and I nearly cried out with memory and longing. I was taken back more than twenty years to a shaft of sunlight in Princes Street Gardens, an Edinburgh fiddler playing under the castle walls, and that same lament for the death of an island chieftain.

I had nothing in our flat to remind me of Starne except an old suitcase I had not replaced. Yet even that piece of battered leather, still plastered with the labels of defunct Scottish railway stations, could release floods of unremitting memories. It was strange how I tormented myself with longing for a place I could have revisited whenever I wished. But I had decided not to return except for those short obligatory visits to my father; it was too dangerous to go back and enjoy it, to risk being seduced once more by an illusory paradise and an archaic way of life. Yet absence and renunciation made it no easier to forget the call of the curlews or the bleating of hill sheep. The Earls Court Road smelt more or less the same from one end to the other, though there might have been minor variations outside the ethnic restaurants. But in a far smaller area at Starne you could smell the freshness of larch after rain, the sharp tang of bog myrtle, the fragrance of heather and thyme and wet bracken. In childhood I had often gone to bed thinking of impossible invented worlds, and in London I sought sleep remembering the details of an

14

unrevisited past, conjuring up the images of a day spent in such and such a place. How persistently I recalled the breakers in Belhaven Bay and searching for hermit crabs in the shallow pools among the sandstone. I inhaled the pungent smell of seaweed and the scent of Scots pines down by the shore. I saw the black shape of a solitary cormorant flying low above the water and in the distance the gannets circling around the Bass Rock and plunging into the sea. Then I walked along the cliffs to the headland and looked westwards at the silhouette of Tantallon Castle, its gaunt impregnable façade standing out against the evening sun.

For eleven years I had been convinced I would sell Starne when my father died, but only now did I ask myself why. It wasn't for reasons of tax debts because I knew we could muddle through with the sale of a few pictures and perhaps one of the lowland farms. It was, I realized suddenly, for reasons of expiation: I was planning to sell in atonement for a single brutal episode eleven years earlier at Oxford. My whole life since then, including my marriage, had been a long act of contrition for a piece of almost atavistic insensitivity. Surely I had now sacrificed enough on my own account without adding my ancestors' house? Besides, I could not seriously argue that it was better or more 'progressive' to bring my children up in London SW5 than to let them run free at Starne with their own tree houses and a world to explore. I recalled the excitement of once finding my father's lead soldiers in an attic cupboard, formidable guardsmen though frequently headless. Was it right to prevent my children from discovering my jigsaw puzzles or my brother's farmyard?

Still sitting at the desk chair, I looked through the study window at the walled garden and the hills beyond, and I knew I could not sell. I imagined the marquee on the lawn, the pin-striped suits of the London auction house, the antique dealers from the southern counties, the transatlantic telephone lines installed for American bidders. The house would be open to all, naked to the most prurient and avaricious of people. I would not have cared much about the sale of the best pictures, Canaletto's views of the Thames, especially if they went to museums, but I would have hated to lose the minor things, the personal objects which remained for ever tied to a single house and a single family. These had been acquired in each generation, loved for their membership of a particular room and used for a real purpose. Removed to an alien place, they would be transformed into useless ornaments.

There was consternation in the library when at last I returned.

'We were becoming somewhat worried about you,' declared Fletcher tersely, looking at his watch.

'Yes indeed,' said Logan with better humour, adding in his ponderous, half-jesting manner, 'We feared something untoward might have occurred and I myself was about to command a search party. Nevertheless,' he remarked, indicating the row of empty beer bottles on the trolley, 'I cannot pretend that the wait has been entirely disagreeable.'

'I'm sorry,' I answered, going over to the fireplace and addressing them from that vantage point. 'It's an important matter and I needed time to make up my mind.' Aware of a mood of expectancy among my listeners, I looked down and caught the glinting eyes of the lawyer. 'In spite of all your persuasive arguments this morning,' I continued, 'I have decided not to sell the house. There is no point giving my reasons which are of no interest to yourselves. That is the decision and it's irrevocable. I know there will be problems with the capital taxes, but we have plenty of time to solve those later.'

16

There was no quick reaction from the group. Logan smiled weakly and scratched the back of his head. The accountant and the junior lawyer looked at the floor and said nothing. Eventually Fletcher said he feared I was making a terrible mistake.

'It'll be the same story all over again,' he added in a more hectoring tone. 'Spend and sell, spend and sell. It's been like this ever since your grandfather asked us to take over your family's affairs. You seem impervious to good advice.'

He had gone too far and I followed him, angrily saying that from that moment he need not bother himself with the affairs of my troublesome family. I was neither nervous nor embarrassed but suddenly filled with a strange fervour, a sense of exaltation, a feeling of the righteousness of what I was doing. By an inappropriate association of images, I recalled my child's bible and saw the picture of Christ driving the moneylenders from the Temple.

When they had gone I rang the bell – a thing I had sworn never to do – that summoned Mr Machale, my grandfather's old butler.

'Will you please ask Mrs Ross to prepare the Oak Room? I expect to be here for a few days.'

It seemed an auspicious moment to move into my grandfather's bedroom with the heavy dark panelling and the Flemish tapestries. My father's room was too closely associated with embittered years and his final illness; moreover, it was not with his sceptical, pessimistic spirit that I wished to begin this enterprise.

Before leaving, the butler said, 'Her ladyship rang, sir, while you were out. She asked if you could return her call.'

For a moment I did not understand whom he was referring to; it seemed unlikely that my mother had rung from Jamaica. And then I realized he meant my wife and

I smiled. It was absurd to think of Ellen as 'her ladyship', a title she certainly would never accept. If Machale or Mrs Ross dared to address her in that way, they would receive impassioned lectures about life in the twentieth century.

The mood of exaltation continued and I grabbed my overcoat and went outside again. A fierce Old Testament sky glowed angrily in the western heavens, making the nearer clouds seem like frivolous puffs of smoke before an uncompromising furnace. But above and to the east reigned the cold blue of the northern sky, its purity gashed by a solitary vapour trail.

I stayed out a long time, delighting in the touch of the grey-pink stone, the tangibility of the old fruit trees and the coldness of the loch water. In my elation I wanted to savour the feeling that they really were mine to preserve and embellish and to hand down to my children and their descendants. Only when dusk came with a still, frost-proclaiming air and I could hear the pheasants roosting in the trees, did I return to my reprieved home.

Chapter Two

i

Nineteen fifty-six is not the first year I remember but the first I recall as a date in which I can place certain events. This was mainly a result of the political crisis which developed into a personal tragedy for my father and culminated in his resignation from Parliament. By the end of that summer, relations between him and my grandfather were deteriorating, though I was not aware of this until the end of the year when they hardly spoke to each other. There was also another, more intimate crisis in the family which was carefully shielded from me, a child of eight, until after Christmas. Nevertheless, I noticed a new atmosphere of tension, especially between my mother and grandmother, and sometimes I caught them whispering angrily to each other. Yet when I approached, they changed the subject or began talking in French. It was not surprising that the first French phrase I learnt was *'pas devant les enfants'*.

That August we went as usual to Ravensmuir, our lodge in the south-west which was later destroyed by fire. If I considered Starne my real home, Ravensmuir was the place of my romantic imagination. It was a smaller house, with few pretensions to either grandeur or comfort, set above a trout loch in the Dumfriesshire hills. Built at the end of the last century with an array of pepperpot towers and 'medieval' turrets, its only function was to house the guests who came in the grouse season. My grandparents had done nothing to change the lodge's character. The bathrooms remained at the end of the corridors with leather firebuckets outside, and the bedrooms had no lamps but a light hanging from the middle of each ceiling. There had been no attempt to create a garden around the house, my grandmother explaining that people could come to Starne to admire her roses but at Ravensmuir they should appreciate the views.

Starne had a long history, as a fortified house, a classical villa and a massive Burn palace of the 1820s. Ravensmuir had no history except as a hostel for several hundred sportsmen from Lord Curzon to the youngest member of the current party, a ruined count from the Baltic. Yet there in the Covenanting hills the lodge was at the centre of Scottish history whereas Starne, grounded in the anglicized East Lothian landscape of neat villages and fertile land, seemed peripheral. The Gordons of Starne had been unheroic Whigs, friends of England and champions of the Union. I used to be ashamed of their history, although I understood why they compromised, for Starne lay on the invasion route and the medieval buildings had been razed on the orders of Henry VIII. But the Gordons of the south-west had never compromised. Some had been Covenanters and others Jacobites, yet all of them had fought for their beliefs and ultimately all had lost. The lands of Ravensmuir had come to the eastern branch through a complicated inheritance, and I cherished them both for what they were and for what they represented as traditional in my country's history. Like many children brought up on Scottish novelists, I accepted the contradictory heritage of both the Covenant and the Jacobite cause. I did so without questioning their merits, identifying myself with the persecuted adherents of both parties. I was on the side of the Covenanters in their hillside conventicles, chanting the psalms even as they were hunted down by the king's dragoons; and I was with the men of Lochaber whose courage nearly won the throne for their Jacobite prince, men who afterwards, when all was lost, hid him in their glens from the English vengeance.

Life at Ravensmuir revolved around two rooms at opposite ends of the basement corridor, the gunroom and the kitchen. The gunroom was never locked during our visits, and I was allowed in to examine the guests' cartridge bags and see what make and colour of ammunition they used. Against the walls stood glass-fronted cabinets with rows of shotguns installed against the baize lining. Most of them were 12-bores but they included a couple of 20-bores and a 'four-ten'. My grandfather had already laid down a schedule for my shooting apprenticeship, so I knew I had to wait three more years before I could handle the 'four-ten'; at fourteen I would graduate to a 20-bore and at eighteen I could expect a pair of adult Purdeys.

Smells from the kitchen often reached the gunroom; they wafted down the corridor of polished flagstones which seemed to reflect recurrent Augusts of hearty eating. Porridge and kippers were the predominant smells of the morning, grouse and grilled fish in the evening. As lunch was invariably a picnic, except on Sundays and rest days, breakfast assumed a paramount place in the day's routine. Large brown dishes of kippers and scrambled eggs lined the hotplates and a smaller bowl of porridge was set aside for my father and grandfather. Our Latvian friend, Count Wolff, felt obliged to taste the porridge on his first morning but he did not repeat the experiment.

'Not quite up my lane,' he explained in an English that was always delightful but never quite accurate.

Breakfast was a prodigious but not an animated meal. My grandfather, who at Starne ate his porridge strolling about the dining room and addressing me as 'wee man', was preoccupied with the planning of the day's sport. Neither my father nor Uncle Fitzroy spoke much, and the other guests seemed cowed by the spirit of earnestness. My grandmother, who also took the shooting seriously and once reproved Count Wolff for wearing turquoise stockings that would scare off the grouse, liked to comment on the season's horse-racing.

'Oh why do people give such silly names to their horses nowadays?' she once exclaimed while reading the race card in the *Daily Telegraph*. 'When you think of all the fine ones in the past, names like Hyperion and Sansovino, it's too nonsensical to call your horse Give-us-a-kiss. Have you ever heard anything so idiotic? The owner must be half-witted.'

The first day of driven shooting took place not on the twelfth but on the fifteenth of August, and on that day the 'guns' paraded on the gravel at nine o'clock, ready to move off in a convoy of Landrovers. In the middle of the morning a smaller party of wives and children set off to join them with rugs and hampers for lunch. In previous years I had been forced to go with them, but this time my father allowed me to travel with the guns. I climbed into the back of the last Landrover with Count Wolff and a couple of labradors, and a keeper drove us high up into the rounded hills to the meeting place. When we arrived, my grandfather was testing the wind with a damp finger while the other guns stood around, smoking or taking mock aim at the skylarks. Three flankers with white flags were standing apart and presently my grandfather went over to give them their positions. Then he came back and told the guns which butts to climb to.

'I'm afraid the younger men have got a bit of a trek,' he said, smiling at Count Wolff. 'Fritz, I'll give you five minutes to get to that top butt.'

'By God,' said the count, following the aim of my grandfather's finger, 'it won't take me a quarter of a jiffy.'

I went with him and we climbed up after one of the flankers. It had rained heavily in the night and the hillside was alive with hidden streams. It was difficult to walk because in places you sank ankle deep into the red and yellow sphagnum moss. But at last we reached the top and I could sit down on a clump of heather behind the turf butt. The count wiped the sweat from his forehead and loaded his gun.

'Let's see how we can polish off these beggars,' he said with a grin.

In previous years I had brought out a toy gun and aimed at the surviving birds as they flew past. But I felt too grown-up for that now and wanted to be useful, marking the grouse as they fell and picking them up at the end of the drive.

They came singly at first, several ignoring the frantic waving of the flankers and flying to the sides out of range of the guns. But with the beaters only a couple of hundred yards off, the coveys began to sweep in, fast and low over the centre of the line. The first seemed to take everyone by surprise and disappeared harmlessly over the Land-rovers. But several fell in the next covey and from then on the bag mounted. Few birds came our way near the summit of the hill, but later in the morning, on the opposite slopes of the glen, the count was given a more favoured position.

It was in the drive before lunch that the women joined us. I was now in my father's butt and his sister, my

Aunt Pamela, was there too, perched on a leather-seated shooting stick. She wore dark glasses and a headscarf knotted under her chin.

'Blast those midges,' she exclaimed, lighting a cigarette. 'Why don't they go away?' She exhaled through her nostrils and turned to me. 'Haven't you brought your cowboy gun so you can go bang! bang! when Daddy misses?'

I scowled crossly at her. My aunt had an annoying habit of making me feel small when I was trying to appear grown-up.

'I'm watching where the grouse fall so I can pick them up afterwards.'

'What a clever boy!'

Her mouth, normally turned down to complain about something, unfolded and smiled. But hers was an uncomfortable smile which was so often sarcastic that I could seldom tell when it was genuine.

Voices shouted 'over!' and my father raised his gun and fired both barrels. The leading bird, spare and stream-lined like a small jet fighter, was transformed instantly into an untidy bundle of feathers.

'Good shot,' said his sister as it dropped into the heather.

My father had little taste for the sport and came out half-a-dozen times a year from habit. Yet he shot competently and a good deal more accurately than one of the foreign guests, a Scandinavian ambassador, whose inept-ness in the neighbouring butt aroused my aunt's scorn.

'I can't think why Papa asks him,' she said. 'He's quite useless.'

'Oh, he's all right,' replied my father, 'though he runs on a bit about the sagas, especially over the port.'

'Personally I find him a grinding bore. And what's more, he's a perfectly hopeless shot.'

24

When the beaters came up and the guns unloaded, she said she could swear he hadn't hit a single grouse. She may have been right, yet the ambassador nevertheless instructed a keeper to bring his dog over and search the ground around his butt.

'It's too ridiculous. He's making poor Morrison waste his time looking for imaginary birds.'

When the keeper picked up a grouse and was heartily thanked by the Scandinavian, Aunt Pamela could hardly control herself.

'Now look what he's up to! He's begun claiming your birds.'

On cold or wet days lunch was eaten in the backs of Landrovers and my grandfather went round with a bottle of sloe gin to invigorate his guests. But this was a glorious day of uninterrupted sun and we sprawled in the shade of a ruined chapel. Near us a couple of keepers were removing the grouse from string-sided game bags and laying them out in rows. When they had finished, the head keeper gave my grandfather the morning total and then joined the beaters' party on the other side of the parked Landrovers.

Uncle Fitzroy sat down next to me, bearing a plate precariously balanced with sandwiches and game pâté.

'Been feeling peckish all morning,' he confided as he began to eat. 'There was a strange fellow in India,' he said, indicating the lines of dead grouse, 'called the Wali of Swat, I think, or maybe it was the Soli of . . . no, anyway, doesn't matter. He had his chaps pick up the guests' empty cartridges and during luncheon they laid them out beside the birds each of them had shot. So you could tell who had done well and who hadn't. Not good form,' he added and then said in a quieter voice, looking across at the ambassador, 'Would have been a bit embarrassing for our blond chum, eh?'

The count was telling a story to the others and we caught the final words. 'So, you can imagine, I felt like an elephant in a china shop.'

Everyone laughed, but I could not tell whether the story was good or just the last sentence. My cousins, Beatrice and Clarissa, were giggling and nudging each other. They were fair-haired and beautiful, even though they were the daughters of Aunt Pamela, and more than ever I wanted to marry Clarissa. But I was in awe of Beatrice, who was two years older than us, especially after what she had told me the day before. We had been in the kitchen garden picking blackcurrants and she had asked if I understood the difference between bulls and cows. Bulls had horns, I replied, and Beatrice had squealed with triumphant laughter. Of course I knew there were other physical differences but I did not realize they served any particular purpose. All day I badgered Clarissa to explain the significance, but she merely went red and said nothing. Yet that night, as I sat eating chocolate in their room after dark, Beatrice told me the whole thing. At first I thought it was a joke and didn't believe her. And then I knew it was the truth because she became so agitated she made me swear not to reveal what I had learnt to my parents.

In the excitement of the morning's shoot I had forgotten her revelation, but now I remembered it and blushed at the memory. All these people in the lunch party, my grandparents, my Aunt Pamela, did they really . . . ? It seemed so ungainly and ridiculous and above all disgusting. I looked at everyone around me but I could not imagine any of them actually doing it.

At the end of lunch a Hillman van drove up the track below us and parked by a gate less than a hundred yards from our party. We watched, silent and astonished, as the doors opened and a large family spilled out on to the hillside. My grandfather was on the whole a tolerant man but he could not stand trippers: he had even put up signs saying 'Beware adders' to frighten them off the moor. He now got to his feet in a controlled rage.

'Would you like me to tell them to push off?' Uncle Fitzroy offered.

My grandfather grunted and shook his head. 'Better let Morrison deal with it.'

The head keeper was summoned and the miscreants pointed out. He swore softly, his indignation matching his employer's, and marched down the track to confront them.

'How maddening,' remarked my grandmother, 'to be bothered by such people. It really is too vexing.'

The adults from the Hillman were now erecting a canvas barricade against the gentle wind, their blond children running into the heather with butterfly nets.

'And what extraordinary clothes they're all wearing! Can you imagine the crassness of wearing orange windcheaters up here?'

We watched as Morrison calmly expelled the intruders, even opening the car door for the reluctant parents, and then my grandfather began allotting the afternoon positions.

I felt sleepy after lunch and lay at the back of the butt in the springy scented heather gazing at the stray clouds gliding overhead. Not wanting to think about Beatrice and what she had told me, I retreated into a fantasy world with my hero and ancestor, Wat Gordon of Lochinvar. This was his country too: his own loch and tower were only a short distance to the west. How often he must have ridden through these hills in his silken doublet and white-feathered hat. People considered him the most reckless blade in the borderlands, and he had fought his way across Scotland and on the continent as well. At

Killiecrankie he had drawn his sword for a king who would not draw his own, riding with Dundee down the Atholl braes to defeat the usurper's force. But when the day was won, Dundee himself had been hit, and his death in the arms of my ancestor had ruined King James's hopes.

Lochinvar's most daring exploit was his elopement with Kate McGhie. Scott and Crockett may have differed over the details but the story was essentially the same: how Wat Gordon had arrived at the girl's house to find her about to marry a man she despised; how he had asked the bride's father as a last favour to be allowed to drink from the loving-cup; and how, when the bride brought it out, he had swung her on to the saddle of his black horse and galloped away. They had stopped briefly at the lochside to be married by the curate of Dalry, and then they had ridden on, ahead of their pursuers, through Dumfries and into England. My grandfather had ridden across the Lammermuirs from Starne to Kelso to propose to my grandmother, but it was hardly a comparable deed because he knew he would be accepted by his bride and her father. Lochinvar's exploit was true love, true romance . . . and then suddenly the magic of the tale was spoiled. There was the heroic ride, yes, and the escape from his enemies – and then? Did Lochinvar and his bride do what Beatrice had assured me all people do on their wedding night?

The routine at Ravensmuir seldom altered. When we returned from the moors, tea and scones were waiting in the hall, set out on linen table cloths. Afterwards the guests moved out to the croquet lawn or took their fishing rods down to the boat house. If it rained, my grandmother arranged various indoor entertainments, usually requiring some kind of acting, to ensure no one was idle.

When the time came, I disappointed my grandfather

by rejecting the shooting schedule he had planned for me. I had turned against the sport and after a reluctant beginning I gave it up. But those summer weeks at Ravensmuir remain a halcyon period for me, and the whiff from a spent cartridge would now revive memories of happiness rather than disgust for the killing. It would remind me of hardy tweed-capped keepers with labradors, of elegant women with cigarette holders in the evening, of men with strong-smelling hair oil who drove Armstrong Siddeley motor cars. The guests were always indulgent to me and seemed light-hearted and confident people with few problems. I realized, of course, that this was not entirely true, for I heard often enough of the illnesses and accidents which befell them. Even my friend the count was not the carefree figure he appeared but a pathetic exile who had lost his estates and had little to hold on to except for a few friendships in Britain. He was a sad man, my mother told me, who spent too much time in his London club hoping for invitations as an extra man at weekend parties.

I know my childhood was not all games and wheelbarrow rides and plum pudding, but it is more difficult to remember the dark things than to recall the sun on the loch at Ravensmuir. It requires an effort to bring back the frustrations and disappointments, the insecurity caused by new challenges, the condescension of adults who patted me on the head and asked me how I liked school. I know it was irritating to be told constantly to brush my hair and practise the piano and sit up at table in case I acquired a back like Richard III or, more drastically, a croquet hoop. It was also annoying – and incomprehensible – to be told not to talk like the nursery maid who said 'perfume' instead of 'scent' and 'pardon' instead of 'sorry'. But compared with later troubles they seem minor irritations. So now do all those fears and anxieties, the fear of the dark or of getting lost in a wood, though they were real enough at the time.

Yet if my childhood had been truly golden, I doubt I would have needed to escape from it so often into my fantasy worlds. These I inhabited when I was in bed and on long car journeys and often in school, so that I soon acquired a reputation for being absent-minded. I spent entire church services in these worlds, and if afterwards my father asked me what I thought of the sermon I was unable to reply. My cousin Clarissa always had a role in my fantasies, sometimes as my queen in a distant oriental kingdom of silks and scimitars and naked women beside oasis fountains. I was surrounded by my generals in the desert and by the women after the campaigns, but Clarissa was the first among them and she was always clothed. More often I was with Lochinvar or in the Highlands in 1745, bringing out my clan for the Jacobite cause; and Clarissa was the lover who tended my wounds after Culloden and helped me escape to the Isles.

ii

Since the spring I had known that in September I would be going south for my first term at boarding school. I seldom talked about it to my parents, although my mother sometimes told me of the exciting things I would be able to do at an English prep school. My father accepted it as a natural destiny, but I knew my mother opposed the idea because I heard her once telling my grandmother it was a barbaric system. I myself went through alternating periods of enthusiasm and dread, becoming naturally more apprehensive as the term approached.

One July morning at Starne I went into my mother's

bedroom and picked up a pair of white gloves. She had worn them the day before at a wedding and they smelt so intensely and wonderfully of her that I stole one and hid it under my pillow. I intended to take the glove to my new school and keep it in my bed to remind me of her, but unfortunately Nanny found it and gave it back. That evening my mother came to say goodnight and sat for a long time on the end of my bed. She had already changed for dinner and wore pearls and drop-earrings and a pale yellow dress. When she was angry her eyes became dark and hard and reminded me of the black-currant pastilles we were given for sore throats. But they had now gone misty under her make-up and she held my hand without speaking. Finally she asked in a low voice why I had taken the glove. I am sure she knew the reason, but on hearing it she burst into tears.

I was still determined to take a memento of her with me, so more than a month later, after our return from Ravensmuir, I took a discarded powder-puff from her waste-paper basket. That night she sat once more on my bed and told me yet again what fun I would have at boarding school. She went on about the sports and the games and the companionship and how I would grow up and learn to look after myself. And then once again she burst into tears and hugged me and made me promise that I would always be hers and would never change.

'Please promise me that, my darling boy. You'll always love me, won't you? You won't be like those stupid boys who think it's sissy to love their mother. You won't change like that, will you?'

And then I too cried and promised I would always love her. I was frightened and bewildered by the intensity of her possessiveness, and I did not understand the reason.

At school I tried not to change and amid the swarm of teasing 'sassenachs' I remained intransigently Scottish.

On my desktop I wrote out my name in defiant letters: Hugh Robert Lindsay Gordon, of Starne and Deloraine in the county of Lothian. And underneath I wrote out the titles of my family and ancestors: Earl of Starne, Viscount Deloraine, Viscount Kenmure, Lord of Lochinvar and Gordonstoun, Baron Ravensmuir, Knight of the Thistle and Companion of the Bath. Beneath them I drew a bold St Andrew's flag, pouring the blue ink between the diagonals, and a lance and three boars' heads from our family arms. I was fined sixpence for defacing the desk but it was worth it.

I could not, however, have survived at that school without compromises. There was no point provoking the sassenachs' derision by using words they did not understand. I remember a conversation about blackberries in which I called them brambles, provoking one of the boys to jeer, 'Typical Scotch cretin to eat the thorns instead of the fruit.'

'In Scotland we call the fruit brambles.'

'That's probably because you can't tell the difference.'

I was furious and scuffled with the boy until I managed to bang his head on the floor. But I never talked about brambles again in England.

I was not miserable that first term and because I thought homesickness was a physical illness I could deny I had suffered from it. Throughout the last fortnight, however, I longed to go home and was counting down the hours until the holidays began. I was to stay three days in my parents' house in Westminster and then take the train north to Starne. When my brother was alive we used to travel by day, Nanny holding us tightly by the hand as she searched for our compartment, my mother supervising the stowing of the luggage in the guard's van. As the train left King's Cross, Nanny moved into her routine of closing the window each time we entered a tunnel to stop the smoke blowing in. My brother and I sat opposite each other by the windows and looked out; we thought the train drivers must be very skilful, much more so than people in motor cars, because they could steer their engines along incredibly narrow rails. After a while Nanny brought out our colouring books and then the picnic basket, but as we went farther north I spent more time looking out of the window. We passed York, which was the half-way point, the North Yorkshire moors and the slag-heaps around Darlington, and then the towers of Durham cathedral. But for me the real north always began farther up, by the flat fields of the Northumbrian coast with black-faced sheep among the rushes and the gulls coming in from Lindisfarne. After that came the red roofs of Berwick and the mouth of the Tweed, and then we were in Scotland, the track running along the cliffs with the sea and the eider duck below. And above everything was the watery northern light and the labyrinth of grey clouds surging away to the east.

That December my mother and I went up alone by the night train and she allowed me to sleep in the top bunk. It was still dark when we arrived and the porters were stamping with cold on the platform. My grandfather's chauffeur was at the station to meet us and he opened the doors of the black Daimler and gave us rugs to keep us warm. I remember the street lamps and the deserted streets, the smell of coal fires from the terraced houses and the broad gentle accent of the chauffeur, the first Scottish voice I had heard since September.

My grandmother, waiting for us in her green Gordon skirt by the fire in the inner hall, ran forward and gave me a long hug. The house was swathed in holly and red ribbons, running up the stairs, draped over mirrors, entwined in the balustrades of the gallery; even the ancestors high above were subjected to a branch of holly on

33

their gilt frames. Breakfast was ready in the dining room and two old ladies were sitting at the table. The profusion of elderly relations was the one, minor drawback of Christmas; my father, who disliked the festivities and stayed at Starne for only a few days, referred morosely to 'the gathering of the clans'. Certainly the house contained several people whom I seldom saw at other times of the year. Two of them were cousins of my grandfather, quiet widowed ladies who divided their days between petit point and games of patience. Another was even older, a great-great-aunt who had once been Mistress of the Robes and now complained about the state of modern curtseying. On Christmas afternoon she used to struggle out of her chair and stand to attention during the Queen's broadcast.

That first day was devoted to reacquaintance. Everyone had to be visited and everything sampled once more. I went to the kitchen, where the cook referred to me as 'the young master' and said how much I had grown. I went out to the orchard, where the gardener chaffed me for using English words and said I had become a wee sassenach. I went to visit my tree house and fixed a plank that had come loose, and I had a go on the swing attached to the great sycamore. I went for a ride on my pony and played with my grandparents' dogs, and finally I went to help my grandmother with the Christmas tree. Decorating the tree was one of the key rituals of the season. My grandmother considered the dark green of the spruce so gloomy that she had it sprayed to look as if it were lightly covered by snow. Then it was carried into the drawing room and installed in the middle of the room. The most boring and uncomfortable part of decorating was winding the tinsel round the trunk and the main branches; only after that had been done could we place the candles and baubles of that year's colour scheme.

Beatrice and Clarissa always came for Christmas and we used to go skating on the loch and tobogganing in the Lammermuirs. There were several days' pheasant shooting, but we didn't go often because it meant standing around for hours on the frosted ground, our feet and hands numb with cold. We much preferred the fox hunts in the Borders which we went to with my grandmother's brother, Uncle Alfred, who lived near Kelso. He was spoken of with much awe as a man who in a single day had killed a stag before lunch, shot a grouse before tea and caught a salmon in the evening. He was also a fine rider who still hunted in his seventies and in his youth had won the United Border Hunts Steeplechase.

Uncle Alfred was a master of foxhounds who had kennels for his pack as well as stables for a dozen horses. I remember his hunters, sleek and enormous, leaning out from their loose boxes high above me, and I remember their buckets painted in his racing colours. A few days before Christmas our ponies were taken from Starne to Uncle Alfred's stables, and twice a week during the holidays we went down to the Borders to hunt them. I still had my Shetland pony, a stubborn furry creature which never failed to exasperate my mother. At the first meet of that winter, in the wide market square at Kelso, she came over to check my girths because the pony had an annoying habit of blowing himself out during saddling. While trying to tighten them, my mother broke a finger nail and cursed and said 'oh, you provoking animal!' And then a foxhound nudged her under the elbow and she cursed it as well. She hated hunting and spent most of the day reading a novel in the Landrover before taking us home.

But my cousins and I loved the atmosphere of the meets, the slow build-up as people rode in from different directions. I loved to watch the hounds with the red-coated huntsman, whose skill and control were so admirable that I sometimes decided I would not be a general when I grew up but a huntsman instead. And I loved to be with the 'field', the loud-voiced men in top hats or bowlers drinking cherry brandy and the veiled women in black, some of them riding sidesaddle. For me there was something strangely alluring about a woman on horseback: often I was struck by the transformation of a dull pedestrian into a mounted goddess. Even my Aunt Pamela was magnificent on a horse, her posture perfect, her breeches stretched so tight that her large behind looked like a couple of drums.

I remember that day in particular because it was the only time I was nearby when a fox was killed. Clarissa and I trotted forward and arrived just as the dismounted huntsman retrieved the brush from the hound pack.

'Please may my cousin have the brush?' she asked timidly, and the man looked up with a smile and said, 'Of course he can, lass.'

He held it up and I was terrified he was going to blood me with the wretched thing. But he merely handed it over with a wink and one of Uncle Alfred's grooms mercifully removed it. I think my uncle subsequently had it cured by a chemist; at any rate, when I returned to Starne for the Easter holidays, the doubtful trophy was waiting for me, sanitized and with a brass ring fixed at one end. But it did not join the other fox brushes on the hook in the nursery passage. I became so fond of the thing that I took it with me everywhere. Perhaps my affection for that pathetic tail turned me against the sport, but there were probably other reasons as well. Anyway, I know I disappointed Uncle Alfred over hunting just as later I was to disappoint my grandfather over shooting.

Christmas Eve was a day of minor rituals, frantic present-wrapping, straightening the candles on the tree, listening to the carol service from King's College on the wireless. In the evening my grandfather invited my cousins and myself to his dressing room to choose a stocking. His invariable joke was to hand us three short socks and then turn away and pretend to leave the room. It was only after we had protested loudly that he came back with a grin and opened his drawer of thick woollen shooting stockings. Beatrice once suggested we should ask my father for the stockings because he was taller and probably had larger ones which could hold more presents. But we never did because we knew that the dressing room visit was one of those ceremonies which could not be disturbed.

At school a few weeks earlier I had been told that Father Christmas did not exist. At first I did not believe it, then I tried not to believe it, but eventually the evidence against him was so great I had to submit. My mother told me that when I was three I had been so terrified by the thought of a large bearded man coming down my chimney that she had had to remove the stocking from the end of my bed and leave it in the passage. I think I was still slightly alarmed in subsequent years, but I never questioned the mystery of how a single man and his team of reindeer could distribute presents to all the children of Britain. And now I knew, as I lay in bed watching the last embers of the fire, that my mother would come in when I was asleep and that there would be no magic about the crammed knobby stocking I would find when I awoke.

On Christmas morning I put on my Gordon kilt and my leather sporran. In these clothes I identified more than ever with Lochinvar, though my father, who scoffed at folkloric traditions, told me that kilts and tartans had not been invented when Lochinvar was alive in the seventeenth century. I knew that it would be one of my last years in a kilt and that when I grew out of it I would have to wear a suit. My grandmother declared it was all right to have kilts in the Highlands but quite wrong for grown men to wear them south of Perth.

Christmas protocol permitted stocking-opening before breakfast but no more presents until after we had returned from church and the entire party had posed on the gravel for a family photograph. We then made for the morning room which was quickly converted into a chaos of ribbons and torn paper.

'What did Santa bring you?' asked Uncle Fitzroy, pressing a ten-shilling note into my hand. 'Put that in your sporran,' he chuckled, 'and don't spend it all on sweets.'

The room echoed with predictable exclamations.

'It's too clever of you. Wherever did you find it?'

'My dear, it's just what I wanted.'

'Darling, it couldn't be more perfect. The exact colour for my bathroom.'

My father moved uncomfortably among the throng, distributing the books he had chosen in a hurry in London and allowing himself to be kissed by his elderly relations. By contrast, my grandfather wandered around beaming and handing out glasses of sherry.

'I was just wondering whether it was time for a little something,' said Uncle Fitzroy.

My grandfather left all the Christmas shopping to his wife. Indeed, his annual contribution was simply to drive into Edinburgh and choose her the largest and most complicated jigsaw puzzle he could find at Jenners. On Boxing Day the puzzle was ceremoniously unpacked in the drawing room and on subsequent evenings he told his guests he would not give them a second drink until they had fitted three pieces.

But that year he had also bought me a present, or

perhaps he had merely found it in one of the attics. He took me over to the writing table and picked up an unwrapped print of Bonnie Prince Charlie.

'He was a foolish young man,' sighed my grandfather, stroking his moustache in contemplation. 'He could have won, you know, if he had taken George Murray's advice. Instead of listening to those blasted Irishmen.'

I hope he didn't notice my disappointment when I looked at the engraving. Above the inscription was no romantic chevalier but an absurd figure in trews, an idiotic-looking man with bulbous eyes and sagging cheeks. I could not believe that this was the Jacobite leader, and as a matter of fact I was right. A long time afterwards I saw the original painting at Dalmeny with a note explaining that for many years it had been wrongly labelled; it was actually a portrait of Lord Dunblane by Hysing.

My grandfather relished his monopoly of carving meat and he enjoyed forcing second helpings of turkey on his widowed relations. He took great delight too in pouring brandy over the Christmas pudding and setting a match to it. After the port there were crackers and the meal ended with the embarrassing sight of old people putting on paper hats. Then we were made to go out of doors and walk off lunch to make room for tea. Until half past four Christmas was a purely family affair, but for tea at least a hundred people were invited, tenants and estate workers with their families and a number of neighbours as well. That was the first time I saw Haldane, who at school and university became one of my closest friends. He was with his father, a bald jovial man who earned my grandmother's derision by wearing a kilt that was too large for him.

'Do look at Jock Haldane,' I heard her say to Aunt Pamela. 'He looks as if he's standing in a hole.'

I was taken over to meet Haldane and we glared silently

at each other. We were about the same height but he was darker and broader and more sure of himself.

'Do you want some Christmas cake?' I asked at last. 'It's got icing and marzipan.'

'I hate marzipan,' said Haldane and then added, 'My house is bigger than this.'

'It isn't,' I answered, 'I've been there.'

The estates of our families 'marched' on the Lammermuirs, the boundary marked by the Deloraine burn, and the houses were no more than five miles apart. But I had never met him before because his father was in the army and they had lived in recent years in Kenya.

'We've got stags' heads on the walls,' he boasted, 'and weapons and armour in the hall. We've got eighty muskets and a hundred and twenty-six claymores.'

'And a whale's tusk,' I said, remembering the story, 'which one of your ancestors bought because he thought it was a unicorn's horn.'

'That type of whale is called a sea-unicorn,' said Haldane furiously.

'But that's not why he bought it. I know because my grandfather told me.'

If we had been anywhere else we would have been fighting by now, but prudence kept us apart until it was time to enter the drawing room for the Christmas tree. For some minutes my father and uncles had been lighting the candles with wax tapers fixed to the ends of bamboo rods. When they had finished, the double doors were opened and the guests surged into the room. They stood around in a circle, gazing at the tree and listening to carols on the gramophone; my grandmother circulated smilingly among them, giving out presents. Grateful that he did not have to stand chatting to people he might not recognize, my father patrolled the tree, a small sponge now tied to the rod which he dipped from time to time into a bucket of water before snuffing out the fading candles.

iii

Although I had promised my mother I would not change, I found that my life was being changed for me. Since I had returned from prep school, long-observed customs and routines had simply been abandoned, unregretted for the most part by me. I no longer went to children's parties or to dancing classes in North Berwick. I no longer had to change after nursery tea before going down to the drawing room to sing nursery rhymes or play an easy card game. Adults no longer treated me as a naive child, giving me Peter Pan explanations about how the world worked. They stopped telling me that thunder was the noise of the clouds fighting and that a rainbow was God's promise not to flood the world again.

In the past I had been allowed to do what I wanted in the mornings but in the afternoons I had been made to go for a walk. With my mother these might have been blackberrying expeditions or visits to the ruined abbey, but with Nanny they were formal walks along the road with definite and pre-arranged goals. There were walks to the home farm past the loch and the factor's house and Lady Emily's cottage, which had been founded as a sewing school by my grandfather's great-aunt. At the farm we looked at the new calves and at the cows in the milking parlour, but I was never allowed to stay long; years later my mother told me that Nanny thought I was showing an unhealthy interest in udders. Another walk was to the village where the goal was the house of Mrs Finlay, a friend of Nanny's who gave me jelly babies which she kept in a china box. She lived near the war memorial which recorded the death of nineteen of the sixty-six parishioners who had volunteered for the Great War. On the green close by was the mercat cross and the spot where four witches had been strangled and burnt in the reign of King James VI. According to my father, however, they had not been witches but terrified old women who had been tortured to confess.

That Christmas I was no longer expected to go for walks with Nanny, and the end of that tradition marked more than anything else the change in my life. I had always thought of Nanny as old, because I knew she had been the nanny for my father and Aunt Pamela and their elder brother, but now suddenly she seemed older still. Perhaps the enthusiasm had left her when my brother died and there was no likelihood of more children to look after. That winter she even grumbled she had not enough work and said it wouldn't be long before my father pensioned her off.

Yet nursery life remained the same for a little longer. Nanny still wore the same reassuring clothes, the white blouse with the grey skirt and cardigan. She still made the same teas for Beatrice and Clarissa and me, the compulsory brown bread and butter to begin with, the scones and shortbread, and the fruitcake and biscuits to end up. She still used the same repertory of immutable phrases, reminding Beatrice that patience was a virtue, telling Clarissa that apple trees would grow out of her ears if she swallowed any more pips, exclaiming that my hair looked as if I had been through a hedge backwards. But she had become more tolerant or perhaps merely more resigned, for she did not go on at us about our table manners; not once, during the entire holidays, did she tell us to take our elbows off the table.

I remember that when Nanny was in a good mood she

used to hum and blow bubbles at bath time; when she was grumpy she grumbled about everything: her laddered stockings, the sloppiness of the nursery maid, the improvements in the prison service. 'Crime pays nowadays,' she remarked once with disgust. 'I wouldn't mind going to prison. They've become like Butlin's holiday camps.' That Christmas I never heard her humming and I was now too old for bubbles blown through fingers; but she went on grumbling.

After supper, when I was in my dressing gown, she sometimes allowed me to climb into her chair in the nursery and brush her hair while she listened to the wireless. I remember an evening after New Year when we heard a play about a wedding.

'Nanny,' I asked ingenuously at the end of it, 'why did you never get married?'

She bent her head and stayed silent for a few seconds.

'I was engaged to be married,' she said at last, 'but my fiancé was killed.'

I put down the hairbrush and crouched in the back of the armchair, wishing I had not been so inquisitive.

'He was my brother Donald's best friend,' she went on. 'Donald and another man were out fishing one day and got into difficulties with the current. My fiancé went out to help them and he too was swept away. All three were drowned. But it's an old story now. I've nearly forgotten it.'

I was too horrified to move, but I could not control my tears and after a while I put my arms around her and my head into the back of her grey cardigan and howled.

'Did you never love anyone else?' I asked later.

'No. God gives you just one person to love and you must marry him if you can.'

'But what happens if one of them lives in Scotland and the other in Brazil? They might never meet.'

'Well it doesn't often happen like that. Men usually prefer to marry women of the same country, which is a blessing. Otherwise we'd all be a funny mixture of brown and white and yellow. And that would not be a pretty sight!'

That night I stayed awake, thinking about Nanny's dead fiancé and crying into my pillow. It was the most terrible story I had ever heard, worse than anything I had read in a book.

I told my mother about the drowning the next day and she said my father had mentioned it when they were first married. It was shortly after the tragedy that Nanny had gone to work at Starne.

'Is it true everyone has only one person in the world he can fall in love with?'

'Not quite true,' said my mother guardedly, 'who told you that?'

'Nanny says it's what God decided.'

'Of course there are some people who do only fall in love with one person. They are the lucky ones.'

She stood up quickly, looked into my father's dressing room and closed the door. Then she sat beside me on the bed, blew her nose and sighed. She was transparently nervous.

'Yes, they are the lucky ones,' she resumed, swallowing. 'Some people never meet the right person and so never marry. Others might think they have found the right one and then discover that the right person was really someone else.'

She paused and looked down and suddenly, with a despairing intuition, I understood what she was going to tell me. Raising her lovely brown eyes and looking mistily at me, she said steadily, with one hand on my forearm, 'Sometimes mothers and fathers discover that they don't love each other after all. Then they become very unhappy

44

living together, so unhappy that it's better for them to separate. Better for everyone, better for the children also.'

'Is that what you're going to do then?'

'Yes darling, I'm afraid it is. We tried very hard to make it work but we didn't succeed.'

I was not conscious of a world crashing on me but only of a numbed feeling followed by a certain anger against my father. My mother was the most beautiful woman in the universe. Why could he not love her?

'What will happen to me?' I asked.

'Nothing important is going to change. This will still be your home – as you know, it always will be. And you will have Granpa and Granny to look after you. And Nanny. And I think Daddy will be living here more now. I shall be in London and I will come to visit you in your new school whenever you want. And you will spend some of your holidays here and some of them with me. I've been thinking of all the exciting things we can do together. We can go ski-ing and visit the Greek islands. I have a friend who has a yacht and I thought that next summer we might go on a cruise with him.'

'Is he the man you're going to marry?'

'No darling, I'm not going to marry anyone. But he's a very nice man, he's called Rupert, and I know you'll like him. He'll teach you to swim under water and use flippers.'

When later I saw my father I was not angry with him. He looked so vulnerable when he had to talk to me that I felt more sorry for him than for my mother. I think I realized even then that it was her decision to leave and that she was going to another man.

'I believe your mother's told you she's going to live in the south.'

'Yes.'

45

'It's a shame of course. We didn't want it to happen. But I'm afraid it can't be helped.'

My father was sitting at his desk in the small study he then had beyond the library. He had just finished reading my school report to me and was now packing tobacco into his pipe.

'As a child one thinks grown-ups organize their lives pretty well and make the right decisions. But they don't, you know, old boy. They make the most infernal mess of things. And it's not really surprising, considering we're just grown-up children.'

He gave me a melancholy smile as he made this bewildering remark and looked out of the window. I saw his lean handsome face in profile, his eyes half-closed and the lines sunk deep in his forehead. His inherent pessimism, I realized later, did not help him to overcome setbacks.

'One of the problems of life is that it has to go on. Your best friend may die, your life may be in ruins, but you've still got to get up in the morning. You've got to keep on living.'

'Some people kill themselves.'

'Yes I know. But only very weak or very mad people. You and I are not like that. We just have to make the best of it.'

He looked so sad that I wanted to go round to his side of the desk and kiss him, but I thought he would be embarrassed. It was horrible to see him so humbled and, impulsively switching culpability, I blamed my mother for making him like this. I had always thought my father strong and indomitable, without weaknesses, a great man who was always right, a man who would one day be prime minister. And now he was reduced to such a state that even a young child could see he was crushed and miserable.

46

Suddenly I recalled certain whisperings I had heard during the holidays.

'Is it true you're going to stop being an MP?'

'It's not up to me, old boy,' he said with a tired resigned smile. 'My constituency party will decide soon.'

'But I thought everyone chooses the MP in elections.'

'They do, but the party chooses its candidate. And some people in Edinburgh are angry with me because I criticized the prime minister and voted against the government.'

'Why did you do that?'

'Because they were wrong. They sent the army to invade another country without just reason.'

He leant across the desk and patted my hand. 'If you like, I will explain the whole thing to you later. But I think it's better not to talk to anyone else about it now. Your grandfather and uncles are also very angry with me.'

I realized only gradually, over a long period, that Christmas that year had been a spectacle for me, a show of artificial jollity and a conspiracy to prevent me from learning the truth until after New Year. Only much later did I learn of the terrible quarrel at dinner when my father had called Eden a liar and my grandfather, who supported the government in the House of Lords, lost his temper and strode from the room. Only later did my mother tell me of the hostility she had suffered from my father's family, the nagging spiteful remarks, the sarcasm, the looks of hatred, all reserved until I was safely out of the way. Later I understood many things, my mother crying at the end of the summer holidays, the change in Nanny and her mood of resignation, the angry conversations in French. Everyone else had known for months about the divorce – I think the marriage had been disintegrating ever since the death of my brother – but it had been delayed for my sake. Everyone had agreed at least on one thing: I could not spend my first term at boarding school knowing that my parents were getting a divorce.

iv

My mother and father had said I would divide my holidays between them, but I spent most of the time with my grandparents and the dog they gave me, a small golden cocker spaniel. When I was at school she was looked after by my grandmother but in the holidays she stayed with me and slept on my eiderdown. The two of us followed my grandmother during her daily visits to the kitchen, the greenhouses and the housekeeper's room. For a time we had a deaf cook who planned the menus with my grandmother by an exhausting process combining sign language, scribbled notes and grotesque mouthing. My grandmother often complained about the staff, especially about the gardeners who never produced a vegetable worth eating, the butler who tyrannized the servants' hall, and a housemaid who smelt so bad that she had to be given special soap.

The administration of the house cannot have been helped by my grandfather's interference. A kindly man with a rash temper, he sacked servants in a rage and then repented and reinstated them the next day. He was particularly bad about remembering names and tended to call all housemaids Linda. Occasionally he failed to recognize people who had worked on the estate for thirty years. When my grandmother remonstrated, he explained that he could always recognize a farmer or a gamekeeper if he found them on a hill wearing a cap and tweed coat; but when he saw them in church, balding men with pink faces dressed in suits, he had no idea who they were.

My grandmother compensated for this ineptness by recognizing everybody on the estate and finding out all about their lives. Between the wars she regularly rode around the farms and cottages, visiting families whenever someone was ill or a baby was born. Although we now went by motor car, the purpose was the same. These visits were an education in several ways, perhaps especially in the field of class distinction. For rural working men my grandmother had sympathy and admiration so long as they did not aspire to a middle-class life. She referred to shepherds and foresters as 'the salt of the earth' and liked them because they led outdoor lives and understood the countryside. But she had only scorn for 'the lower orders' who became socially ambitious, the farmers' wives who wore high heels and bright clothes in the country. She couldn't bear people who would have been glad to exchange their moorland cottage for a bungalow in Dunbar.

Views were a constant preoccupation of my grandmother's, houses often being judged less by their appearance than by the view from their windows. Her favourite place was 'the Countess's view', named after her husband's grandmother. You reached it by a long sloping drive through the woods to the east of Starne and at the top my Victorian ancestors had built a summer house of thatch and birch logs. From its windows you could see the whole coastal plain from Prestonpans to Dunbar and beyond it the islands of the Forth and the coast of Fife.

In bad weather my grandmother was resourceful about entertaining me inside the house. There were various Jacobite novels which she read aloud and several board games which she set up on the card table. She even tried to share my interest in sport and sometimes we watched a test match together. I remember how she admired the

West Indian cricketers and used to refer to Garfield Sobers as 'one of nature's gentlemen'. They were fine physical specimens, she declared, but one had to admit there was something slightly absurd about the pale palms of their hands.

Many wet afternoons were absorbed by canasta, which we sometimes played by ourselves and sometimes with Uncle Fitzroy and my grandfather's secretary. I remember little about the game except that whenever she played the nine of diamonds my grandmother called it 'the curse of Scotland'. I don't think I ever asked the reason for this melodramatic title, but many years later I learnt that it was on that card that the order for the Glencoe massacre was given. If my father entered the morning room during a game, he usually said something like, 'Good heavens! Are we in Sunningdale?' so that for a long time I thought of Sunningdale as a place where no one did anything except play canasta. But my grandmother told me it was also a popular game in the Borders; the area around St Boswells, apparently, was full of canasta players.

Meals at Starne had a certain predictability. My grandfather would sample a dish and then look across with a pained expression at his wife. 'But my dear Betty,' he would say, 'the soup is stone cold,' or 'these potatoes are completely overcooked,' or 'this mutton is quite inedible. One might as well be eating shoe leather. We must change butchers.' Once, when the deaf cook produced an innocuous white sauce, he accused her of trying to emulate 'greasy French cooking'. He felt better after making these complaints and might then turn to me and talk about the First World War or about his time in India as a viceroy's ADC. There was often an excursion into Scottish history; he loved to describe macabre incidents such as the Douglas Larder or the Black Dinner or the murder of a Scottish king in the Black Friars' monastery at Perth.

'. . . And when they heard the clash of weapons, King James sprang to his feet to lock the door. But there was a traitor in their midst who had removed the iron bolts. The brave Catherine Douglas thrust her arm through the metal loops and held off the attackers while the king tore up a plank from the floor and jumped into the vault below. But they soon broke the arm of the poor woman, who was known afterwards as Catherine Barlass or Kate-bar-the-gate, and burst into the hall. The king might have escaped for there had been a way out of the vault through a narrow hole to the open air. But because he used to lose his tennis balls down that hole, he had ordered it to be blocked up three days before. And there Robert the Graham and his murderers caught him and stabbed him to death while the queen screamed in the hall.'

'Oh, why must you always tell such doleful tales?' my grandmother complained once.

He gave me a wink and said, 'Because, my dear, Scotland has had a most doleful history.'

'All these odious traitors . . .'

'We were betrayed in every generation from the treachery of Sir John Menteith to the cowardice of Murray of Broughton. We are a nation of traitors.'

'And heroes,' I added.

'Yes,' he smiled, stroking his moustache, 'perhaps a few heroes.'

It was better, I felt, to have a mixture of brave men and villains than to have neither, like the English. I had not yet read about Drake and Hawkins but I knew Napoleon had called England a nation of shopkeepers.

My grandmother's views on Scottish history were coloured by her theory of good and bad blood. Once a family acquired 'bad blood', she argued, it was doomed, its members tainted for generations, its evil deeds attributable to this appalling birthmark. According to her, the

Frazers and Campbells had notoriously bad blood and she used to quote with approval Charles II's remark that 'there never was trouble brewing in Scotland but that a Dalrymple or a Campbell was at the bottom of it.'

My grandfather derided the theory.

'The Campbells are like us Gordons, my dear, spread all over the place and only tenuously connected. You cannot blame the Campbells of Cawdor or Breadalbane for something their kinsmen did in Argyll.'

'I'm not talking about clans but about families. I know about bad blood and I've seen it reverting hundreds of times. One can never get away from it.'

When I was nine it was suggested I should have cricket coaching in the Easter holidays. My grandfather said he wouldn't hear of the scheme and resolved to tackle the job himself. He was barely seventy, he declared, and could still bowl a cricket ball.

He embarked on the task with characteristic zest, taking me that afternoon to Edinburgh to buy my first cricket bat. After a good deal of measuring in the sports shop, he chose a size four, a pair of pads and various other equipment. At home he poured linseed oil on to the face of the bat, warning me it was important to avoid the splice, and then left it to dry on an urn in the garden. When it had dried there was the ritual of 'playing it in' by knocking an old ball up and down so that the bat soon lost its clean new appearance. After more oil, another drying and a further ceremony of playing it in, we were ready to begin. My grandfather strode out to the middle of the lawn and set up the stumps. That first year he bowled underarm and, when I missed, the ball stopped only a few yards behind the wicket. The following season he bowled overarm, a curious classical action such as one sees in old prints in which the left arm is barely raised. The ball then travelled farther and we had to persuade

Uncle Fitzroy to act as wicket-keeper or build a barricade of garden chairs. Later, when I had acquired a larger bat and was hitting the ball quite hard, my grandfather bought a practice net to reduce the time wasted searching for the ball among the flower beds.

His bowling instructions were straightforward. 'Concentrate on line and length. Don't try to bowl too fast. Don't pretend to be Larwood.' The batting instructions were more complicated; there were so many things to remember that I was almost bound to forget something. 'Keep your head down', he exhorted; 'Pick your bat up straight'; 'Foot to the pitch of the ball'. He himself had been an excellent player and had scored a half-century in the Eton–Harrow match. He abhorred cross-bat shots and inelegant swipes to leg, and when I played them he used to shout in exasperation, 'Less of the agricultural if you please!'. If I persistently failed to play the correct shot, he would march down the pitch in his Eton Ramblers cap and demonstrate the backward defensive or the cover drive. Towards the end of our sessions we played a private game in which, according to the quality of my shots, he awarded me runs. If I mishit a drive and the ball disappeared to leg off the edge of my bat, he shouted 'Harrow!' and refused to give any runs. If the ball struck my pads, he cried 'Howzat!' and turned round to appeal to an imaginary umpire.

There were other things my grandfather wanted to teach me apart from cricket. Even in his seventies he spent most of his day out of doors and he wanted to show me how he drained his fields and managed his woodlands. Our tours of the estate were hazardous affairs for he was a famously bad driver and frequently drove his Landrover into a ditch. We might be driving over the moor, my grandfather peering out of the windows, when suddenly he would exclaim, 'By God! Are those blackcock down there?' and within seconds the jeep was lying on its side in the heather.

Like many hunters, he loved birds and animals even when they were not targets for his gun. He used to take me to see the waders in Aberlady Bay and sometimes we went out in a boat to watch the gannets on the Bass Rock. In the Easter holidays we listened to birdsongs in the woods and I remember the day he taught me to identify the soft rippling song of the willow warbler. He also tried to teach me how to fish but I think he realized early on that it was a waste of his time. While casting on the loch at Ravensmuir, I hooked him painfully in the back of the neck and his appetite for the lessons diminished.

Enthusiasm for my shooting career, however, remained strong in spite of my reluctance to start it. Between the middle of August and the end of January he had fifty or sixty days' shooting and even out of season he could keep in practice; he was quite content to blacken his face with burnt cork and sit all day in a cornfield to shoot a couple of hundred pigeons. He was thus unable to understand why I found the idea unappealing. When I timidly re-marked that I did not like killing things, he grunted, 'In that case you should become a vegetarian and wear plastic shoes.' My attitude put him in such a bad mood that I finally succumbed. I was fourteen, too old for the 'four-ten', so I began my shooting career with a 20-bore aimed at clay pigeons. I then advanced to real pigeons and spent several afternoons shooting at them in the Starne woods. The entire bag, twelve birds shot in as many hours, was handed over to the cook who baked them in a pie. Nanny, who had retired to Dunbar some years earlier, saw this pathetic pie in the kitchen when she was paying a visit. 'Poor wee things,' she remarked sadly. 'It's a shame isn't it, to be born into this world just to end up in a pie like that.' I agreed with her unreservedly and refused to try a mouthful of it at dinner that evening.

One day my grandfather arranged for a keeper to take me out to the woods and said he wanted me to come back with a brace of cock pheasants. So I went out on a bitter January afternoon with my spaniel and a dour grim-faced man called Helm. We saw a roe deer in the park and a number of hen pheasants but no cocks. I was in an impatient disgruntled mood and, as the darkening began, I became determined to shoot my first pheasant and present it to my grandfather. We had turned for home near the loch when Helm pointed to a tree and I saw a pheasant roosting in the branches. I could not shoot a stationary bird so I decided to make a noise and fire as it flew away. Suddenly, however, the pheasant flapped its wings and I raised my gun and pulled the trigger. As it fell to the ground I realized with horror that the bird had not moved at all and I had broken one of the cardinal rules of sportsmanship.

'It was flying, wasn't it?' I asked nervously.

'Och, it hadna moved far,' replied Helm.

My misery was compounded by the discovery that the bird was in fact a hen. I was too ashamed to tell my grandfather I had shot a roosting hen pheasant, so I left the creature behind a tree in the garden and told him we had drawn a blank. Later that evening I took a torch and a spade and went out into the dark to bury the wretched thing. In the night I became sentimental and miserable, tormented by anthropomorphic visions of the pheasant's ruined family.

Two days later, when I thought the incident was over, my grandfather said, 'I'm told you shot a pheasant which cannot be traced in the larder. Do you know what happened to it?'

'I'm afraid I buried it.'

'You what?'

I described the unsporting shot and the consequent guilt, explaining that I thought the only decent thing to do was to bury it.

'But what's the earthly use of that? Once it's dead, one might as well eat it. Can't make much difference to the pheasant.'

'I know but I had to do it.' More boldly I added, 'I'm afraid I don't like shooting and I want to give it up.'

'But you've only just started.'

'I've done enough to know I don't enjoy it.'

'My dear boy, everyone goes through stages when they become confused and don't know what they want. Just keep practising and you'll learn to like it. Morrison says it's going to be a capital year for grouse.'

But I was obdurate. I didn't want to leave the matter undecided so that it would be brought up again and the arguments repeated. My grandfather reacted angrily in his disappointment and remarked that burying the pheasant was the most pansy thing he had ever heard.

That episode ended the close relationship I had had for many years with my grandfather. He was nearly eighty then, our cricket games were over, and I no longer enjoyed bumping around in his Landrover inspecting trees. We still talked about history and he liked to recite Scott and Stevenson to me, but we were both aware that I was not the grandson he should have had. When he was eighty-one and I was seventeen, he made a last appeal to me.

'I think you'll find time hanging heavily in middle age unless you take up shooting again.' And because it was such an absurd remark, and because he was old and I loved him, I took up a gun once more and walked along the side of a hill at Ravensmuir. I hit nothing and never did it again.

For ten years my grandparents were more important

in my life than my mother and father. I saw both parents during the holidays and sometimes one of them at half-term, but usually only for brief periods. They always seemed to have long travels and complicated plans which did not fit in with my own. My father had been forced to resign from the House of Commons after Suez and he had returned to his old job as a lecturer in classics at Cambridge. As he was writing a book about the Greeks of Syracuse, he spent much of the university vacations in Sicily. But he always made a point of coming to Starne for a few days during the holidays and of spending a week at Ravensmuir in August. I am sure he regarded these visits as tours of duty to please me and my grand-parents. He made an effort to talk to his father about matters such as winter wheat and the new plantations, but I could see that they bored him. The brutal ending of his parliamentary career appeared to have concluded his interest in politics and the modern world, and his mind had retired to an earlier civilization.

My father often seemed an older spirit than my grand-father. His detachment and lack of enthusiasm made it difficult for him to understand a child's world and he was uncomfortable even during our cricket games. Talking to me about books made him feel more at ease and he gave me his childhood collections of Weyman and Henty. When I had measles he read Sherlock Holmes stories during winter afternoons at Starne; in the middle of each tale we used to guess the murderer and the means of murder and write them down on pieces of paper.

I remember him standing in the morning room on the day before I went to Eton. He had poured himself a whisky and soda and was looking gaunter and more uncomfortable than ever. When I said I was going up for my bath, he gulped at his drink and asked me to stay for a couple of minutes. We sat down in armchairs on opposite sides of the fireplace and then he said abruptly, 'I expect you know all about sex.'

'Yes, I think so,' I replied, though in fact I had only a biological knowledge of the means of reproduction.

After a pause he asked, his eyes fixed on the carpet, whether I knew about homosexuals. I had never heard of them but I imagined they were people I ought to have known about. They sounded Greek and I wondered if they might have been philosophers.

'I've heard of them,' I answered, 'but I can't remember exactly who they were.'

I could see what it cost my father to explain. He swallowed some more whisky and began to move his hands about in a disconcerted way.

'Well, it's not their fault of course. In fact it's bad luck, just the way they are made. But they're men who like other men, or rather they prefer men to women and therefore don't marry.'

This seemed pretty harmless and I couldn't see why he was making such a performance.

'Is Uncle Fitzroy one?' I asked.

'No, no, good God no. Most bachelors are perfectly normal people who just decided not to get married. Homosexuals, or queers as they're sometimes called, are rather different. They like going to bed with other men.'

'Whatever for?'

'Well, just like married couples sleep in the same bed. Anyway,' he went on hurriedly, 'a certain amount of it went on at Eton in my day and I daresay it's still about. So you may need to watch out. You're reasonably good-looking and someone might sort of . . . . Well, anyway, there it is. What time's your train in the morning?'

I would have liked to ask him more but he plainly hoped the conversation was over. I wanted to know how it could possibly be like married couples in bed if men

58

couldn't have babies. When it was eventually explained to me at school by Haldane, I couldn't believe that people did such things. Later I understood what my grandmother meant when she said in a low deliberate tone that so-and-so was 'one of them'. She often invited effeminate young men to look at the pictures and furniture at Starne. Did they really, I wondered, practise this bizarre and appalling activity?

My grandparents did everything they could to entertain me and invited friends to stay so that I was not lonely. But I think they realized how much I missed my mother, and once I overheard my grandmother discussing it with Aunt Pamela: it was disgraceful, she said, that Angela should take such little interest in her son. That I saw much less of my mother than she had promised was true, but I knew she thought of me because she sent so many postcards. I kept them and still have them: cards from Casablanca, Capri, St Jean de Luz, Chicago and dozens of other places; cards that wished me luck in cricket and exams, cards that always told me something of the places where she was staying. 'It's so hot here,' she wrote from Orissa, 'that you can grow bananas and coconuts.'

My mother was thirty-one, ten years younger than my father, when they separated. I think she thought of her twenties as a lost decade when she had been denied the amusements enjoyed by her sisters and younger friends. She had never 'come out' or had a dance because of the war, and within two years of VE-day she had married a man who behaved as if he were already middle-aged. After leaving him, her one aim was to compensate for those wasted years and to experience as much of life as possible. She did not marry Rupert the yacht-owner but she travelled with him around the world. I did go on his yacht once and he did teach me to swim under water. But my mother was wrong when she said I would like him; I knew instinctively he was what my grandfather would have called a 'bounder'.

She stayed in London for a year or two and then moved to Paris where she studied painting. At the beginning of my holidays she came back to London and we stayed for a few days at the house of one of her sisters. In July we had a fortnight together. The first year she rented a house at Frinton but the place bored her: there was little to do except walk along the beach and she refused to swim in the North Sea. Some friends occasionally visited us, bringing picnic hampers in a sports car, but when they had gone she became still more restless. Even I was bored and wanted to go to Scotland; I was too old to build sandcastles and, after fox-hunting in the Borders, it was difficult to enjoy donkey rides along the beach.

After that we spent the annual fortnight abroad. There was one visit to Venice but in other years we went to villas at Ischia or Formentor or Juan les Pins. I think I experienced more misery during each of those fortnights than in all the rest of the year. I looked forward to them too much, desperate to see my mother again, and wanting to talk to her all the time. But we were always surrounded by other people: her cosmopolitan friends who spoke several languages, bronzed languid women in bikinis, smooth dark men in bermuda shorts who drove two-seaters and were excellent water-skiers. Some days I saw little of her. She rarely got up before eleven and then went down to the sea to swim and sunbathe. We had late lunches and long siestas, and the evenings were usually devoted to parties and visits to a nightclub. I passed much of the day reading and idling around the local hotel, playing table tennis with people I didn't know. I used to go into my mother's bedroom when she was putting on her make-up before a party, and I was hurt because I could see she was excited and didn't mind if I was left alone in the villa with the servants. Sometimes I was allowed to go out with the others to a restaurant or a trattoria, but one of them always drove me home before they went on to the nightclub. When I was fourteen I went to a couple of parties with them. I remember a villa near Antibes, a floodlit pool and Moroccan servants carrying trays of champagne and caviar. As we arrived my mother told me in a whisper to call her by her Christian name in front of other guests and she introduced me all night as Hugh, never as 'my son Hugh'.

There was no one there of my age and nobody who wished to talk to me. I stood about watching men greet my mother with kisses on both cheeks. I don't know if they were friends or lovers or merely people she had met the previous evening, but I hated them all. Later on I saw her sitting among the oleanders in the garden, laughing with a man who had a hand on her knee and an arm around her neck. I was so jealous I thought of hitting him or throwing a glass of wine in his face, as Lochinvar would have done. But I went down to the sea instead and sat at the end of the diving board gazing at the lights on the distant fishing boats. I wanted to die. I loved my mother and wanted to be with her, but it was obvious she preferred the company of other people. She was a young woman who wished to appear even younger and she didn't hide the fact that a teenage son was an encumbrance. I looked up at the stars and swore I would never again spend a summer holiday with my mother.

Chapter Three

i

At Eton Haldane seemed to be one of those boys who achieve a pre-eminence at school which they are unable to repeat in their subsequent lives. Yet he swaggered through university with the same arrogance and self-assurance. He smoked and drank too much to row for Oxford as he had rowed for Eton, but he gained a reputation as a debater and a politician. There was a recklessness and flamboyance about him which attracted women. In an age when most undergraduates were trying to outflank each other on the Left, Haldane remained an uncompromising conservative. He kept his hair short, wore tweed suits and blazers, and did nothing to modify a resonant upper-class accent.

He made his name in the Union and the Conservative Association, but he also spoke in the less congenial setting of the Balliol Junior Common Room. During vehement exchanges between communists and Trotskyites over some international issue, Haldane, the only conservative at the meeting, would intervene with a disdainful well-delivered speech criticizing both factions. Yet it would have been easier to applaud him had he been less provocative and contemptuous of his opponents. His dislike of long-haired denim-clad revolutionaries was not only political. He promoted a nasty class-based antagonism, jeered in private at their origins and referred to them as 'grubbies' or 'the great unwashed'. He also enjoyed dreaming up schemes to bait the leftists. After one club dinner he persuaded his black-tied friends to sing 'Land of Hope and Glory' outside the Junior Common Room until they were chased from the college.

In our second Michaelmas term Haldane was running for one of the Union offices. He spoke in most of the debates and spent other evenings in the Union bar trying to charm potential supporters. It was easier to find conservatives there than in our college. I was not much interested in politics but I sometimes listened to debates and I liked the Victorian library. I was sitting in one of its leather armchairs one evening when he came in.

'I thought I would find you skulking in here. Come and have a drink. I'm fed up with illegal electioneering.'

We found a table at the end of the crowded bar.

'So how's life at the top?' I asked.

'Hard,' he replied with a complacent smile, 'devilish hard. My damned tutors are complaining about my lack of work. How can I work when I have to fight these elections?'

He was also standing for the presidency of the Conservative Association and had signed me up as a member so that I could vote for him.

'I hear you've been wenching,' he said suddenly with a grin.

I shrugged and attempted to change the subject.

'Come on,' he persisted, 'you can't deny it. Middleton told me about the bet.'

I wish I had said then that I was ashamed of the matter

and didn't want to discuss it. But I smiled weakly and let him go on.

'He said it took you only forty-eight hours. Not bad, I grant you, but she's nothing to write home about. Easy on the eye, maybe, but tarty. Looks like a shop assistant.'

'She doesn't,' I answered. 'In any case, she's an extremely nice girl.'

'Yes, but common. Not what I should have expected of you.'

'Look, it was a stupid bet, we were very drunk and I wish it had never happened.'

I had been trying to forget that Saturday evening at the Gridiron Club when Middleton and I had been drinking and laying bets on anything that came into our heads: the Ashes, the Hennessy Gold Cup, the following year's American elections. It was ladies' night at the Grid and Middleton had pointed to a blond girl in the corner.

'I'll wager you a magnum of champagne you can't get that filly into bed before this time next week.'

'But I don't even know who she is.'

'Her name's Janet Black and she's at St Anne's,' said Middleton. 'And frankly I'm being generous with the time factor. She strikes me as a pushover.'

I wish I had not accepted the bet, or competed for it, or later claimed the champagne. But I did all three. I met her by chance at a party two days later and we had a short and loveless affair. Annoyed with Middleton, bored by the girl and disgusted by my own behaviour, I ended it within a fortnight. Janet was understandably bewildered, hurt and angry, and wrote me a series of devastating letters. On discovering that I had a girlfriend in London with whom I was supposed to be in love, she approached me at a party and threw red wine in my face.

Haldane was explaining why he preferred having affairs with debutantes rather than undergraduates.

'The problem with brainy girls is that they like to discuss important things in bed. What did Janet what's-her-name want to talk about? Nietzsche?'

I didn't answer and he stood up to greet a political ally. I was about to leave when a girl at the next table turned around and addressed me in an American accent.

'May I have a few words with you?'

'By all means.'

She had long dark hair, parted down the middle, and nearly black eyes. Her face was thin with an intense determined look which Haldane would have rejected as too 'brainy'.

'When two upper-class Englishmen,' she began, settling into the chair vacated by Haldane, 'talk to each other in loud upper-class voices, it's difficult to avoid overhearing what they say.'

I said uncomfortably, 'I'm sorry if we disturbed you.'

'It wasn't the braying noise you guys make that disturbed me. It was what you said that made me want to throw up.'

I felt she was being unfair as well as offensive. It was Haldane, after all, who had done most of the talking.

'Look, it was a private conversation. I don't see what business it is of yours.'

'Oh don't you? Well let me introduce myself. My name is Ellen Hartman.'

'Yes?'

'I'm at St Anne's. My neighbour and closest friend is Janet Black.'

'Oh.'

'Is that all you can say?'

She looked at me intently, her mouth creased with contempt.

'I don't understand people like you and that jerk Roddy

Haldane. Who do you guys think you are? A couple of eighteenth-century toffs having sport with the serving wenches? Trying to bring back the *droit de seigneur*? Is that right? Women don't exist for you as real people, do they? We're just creatures you hunt down and make us open our legs when we're caught.'

Her anger had defeated her sarcasm and her look of glaring hatred reminded me of a Red Indian squaw in a child's picture book.

'Why don't you calm down instead of becoming hysterical? Lots of people have casual affairs.'

'Don't tell me to cool it, man. Do you think Janet was calm when she saw how you'd humiliated her? She told me all about it. She said she'd slept with some guy on the first date and realized it was a dumb kind of thing to do. He was some sort of lord, she said, but he was gentle and considerate and he didn't seem to be interested in just a one-night stand. Anyway, she was relieved when you came back the next day or the one after, because she thought it meant you were genuinely fond of her. And she had become crazy about you. I don't know why. You strike me as weak and immature and living in the wrong century.'

'Well, I may be all those things, but I do regret it. I am sorry it happened.'

'That's mighty big of you,' she said mordantly. 'Very consoling for Janet. Can you imagine what it feels like to really fall for a guy and then discover that he just wants to screw you for a few nights? No passion, no meaningful relationship, just a dozen orgasms and your quota's up. And then on top of that, to read in some goddamn gossip column that the Honourable Hugh whatever-you're-called is having a romance with Lord So-and-so's daughter, Miss Moronic Debutante. It must make one feel pretty good huh?'

66

She leant towards me and the Red Indian look returned to her eyes.

'But thank God there's one thing she doesn't know.'

'What's that?'

'What I learnt tonight. That you did it all for a bet. That's got to be the most disgusting thing I ever heard. I don't know why you don't feel sick just looking at yourself in the glass.'

Well I did, more or less, after that conversation. A week later term ended and I went up to Starne for the holidays. My grandmother had died earlier in the year and Christmas was a dismal, largely masculine affair. There were one or two parties and Haldane invited me to a dinner to celebrate his election as president of the Conservative Association. But I refused every invitation. The only time I saw Haldane during the vacation was on Christmas Day in the Episcopal church in Haddington.

I had always hated criticism and used to brood on it for longer than it generally deserved. I thought constantly of Ellen Hartman's lecture and of the events that had prompted it, lying awake at night, my face hot with shame. In fact, I became ashamed not only of my treatment of Janet Black but of my entire Oxford existence. We led a ridiculous life, I realized, a caricature of past decadence, a life of unending parties and club dinners, of port-drinking and pompous toasts. Our arrogance was without *angst*, our boorishness unrepentant, our élitism based on repellent assumptions of class superiority. We saw ourselves as guardians of tradition, a thin line of elegant cavaliers standing against the red tide of the sixties. Haldane, Middleton and the rest talked of their political futures as if parliamentary success were ordained; their heroism would help save the nation.

I fretted incessantly about what had happened to my life. People used to say I was sensitive, too much so, but nothing could have been more insensitive than the life I led at Oxford. At school I had been different. I had not been a member of the loud-mouthed beer-drinking rowing set; I had not been one of those boys who strode about, their careers already graphed out, confident of a destiny conferred by status. I was considered a reformer, a mild rebel, above all a questioner. Once I was summoned by the headmaster to explain why in chapel I had refused to sing 'I vow to thee my country'; I said I loved the music but I could not stand the jingoism of the verses. I had not accepted confirmation as an inevitable ritual to be undergone; I needed to be sure of my faith and I had been prepared to opt out at the last moment. I remember an evening service in summer with the sunlight coming through the stained-glass windows; and I looked up at the chapel roof while the choir sang 'Nisi Dominus' and asked myself, 'Would they have built all this if they hadn't been sure?'

I had often wondered whether the school should be abolished. Its merits seemed minor in comparison with the resentment it provoked among people who did not go there and the unearned self-confidence it donated to those who did. Yet there were moments when the place seemed to justify itself, moments of exaltation when we all sang 'Jerusalem' and it was possible to believe that the great schools were not just breeding grounds of snobbery and arrogance, that they did have some connection with faith and honour and civilization.

And now I was able to live with the snobbery and the arrogance. I had repudiated the ideas of my childhood and schooldays; I was a friend of men who spoke of girls as fillies and wenches. Yet at school I had never thought of sex as separate from love and I despised boys who had. I had always had romantic notions of love, both during the years when it had been confined to letters and holiday kisses, and later when it had become more physical and more complicated. From the age of fifteen I had become infatuated with two or three girls a year and had regarded them in an absurdly romantic light. To each I had sent poems, my own and other people's, and to each I had dedicated a sentimental song composed on the piano. I used to identify them with the violin concerto I revered at that moment and gave them their respective records, a series that began with Brahms when I was fifteen and ended four years later with Sibelius. There was a spell in each concerto which seemed to epitomize the emotional tension in my love: Campoli drawing his bow through the soaring last notes of the Mendelssohn, the lyrical adagio of the Bruch, Menuhin's late cadenza in the Elgar. I used to wait for the passages and then picture the girls' faces, radiant and intense, reflecting the ardour of romantic love.

Teenage passion was a frantic thing, with the sleepless nights, the nervous telephone calls, the dance floor fervour and tentative fumbling, the tumultuous scenes of breaking up, the tears and letters of recrimination. Yet sometimes I recognized that I was not so much in love with a particular girl as obsessed with all women. I remembered girls I had adored at tea parties as a small child, nannies standing behind our chairs, or at the seaside, or even in church when I caught the eye of one in a nearby pew. At primary school an ugly scabrous boy called Hoggett had jeered at me when I intervened to prevent him bending back the fingers of Kirstie Munro. 'Always on the girls' side,' he had mocked with a derisive spit. It was true and I was proud of it. I was on their side, not because I thought I resembled them or enjoyed doing the same things, but because I liked them and wanted to be their protector.

Ten years later I had not changed. Within twenty-four

hours I could love the blond hair of a thirteen-year-old child, the bust of a shop assistant and the sinuous walk of a woman of my mother's age; and with all of them I could imagine being in love and having them in my arms. Sometimes I merely had to meet a girl and talk for ten minutes before experiencing an urge to make sacrifices for her and tell her I loved her. I dreamt a lot about women, passionate dreams of girls I knew and of whom I thought differently thereafter, almost as if I really had made love to them; and dreams of girls I did not know, non-existent women who disturbed my nights and left me with a sense of loss when I awoke.

ii

I returned to Oxford in January and resigned from the Gridiron, the Conservatives and a couple of self-regarding dining clubs. On the second day of term I walked up the Banbury Road to the dismal blocks of Janet Black's college. She was not in her room so I sat on a radiator in the passage and tried to compose a contrite and friendly note. After a few minutes the next door opened and Ellen Hartman came out carrying a kettle.

'Jesus!' she exclaimed, 'what are you doing here?'

'I came to see Janet.'

She looked at me uncertainly. 'I think she went to the library.'

'Well, I'll just leave her a note then.'

Ellen walked barefoot up the passage with the kettle. Her black dress of crushed velvet nearly reached her toes.

'I'm making some coffee. Do you want some?'

'That's very kind of you. Why not?'

Her room smelt of spices and exotic fumes; little cones

of sandalwood were glowing in the ashtrays. On the floor three men and a girl sat crosslegged listening to the gramophone.

'Hi everybody,' said Ellen. 'This is Hugh. And these are Boris, Luke, Mark and Gwendolen.'

'Hello.'

'Hi man,' said Boris.

'Peace,' said Luke.

'Why don't you sit down,' said Ellen, 'while I make the coffee?'

Regretting my acceptance of her offer, I sat awkwardly in the narrow space between Boris and Mark. I wanted to go; I didn't even like coffee very much. All three men had long hair and wore jeans and dyed tee-shirts. I felt they were looking curiously at my tie and grey flannels.

'Do you dig Dylan?' Mark asked me after a while.

'Sorry?'

'Do you like Bob Dylan?' he translated. 'What we're listening to.'

'I'm afraid I don't know much about him.'

'Christ, man, where are you at?' said Boris.

I listened to the nasal American voice: it whined, 'The sun's not yellow, it's a chicken,' but I didn't dare ask what this was supposed to mean.

Ellen handed me a mug with an indulgent smile. She was amused, I think, at the sight of me in such a gathering.

'Luke's a crazy cat,' Mark said, pointing to the figure opposite with his eyes closed. 'He plays bass.'

I thought this was a reference to baseball and it surprised me. Luke didn't look as if he could stand up, let alone wield a baseball bat.

'Boris is drums,' he went on. 'I play lead and Gwendolen sings. Ellen should sing too. She's got a good voice, like Joan Baez you know. Only she's too much into politics. Heavy like.'

71

I had already noticed a poster of Che Guevara on the wall opposite and another of some guerrillas carrying a banner with the word *Venceremos*! Revolutionary politics also dominated the bookshelves, Mao, Marx and Lenin each receiving a section of their own. Less austere hints of Ellen's life were revealed by the guitar in the corner and the Indian silk scarves draped over the mirror.

'She's not quite a commie,' said Mark with a smile. 'Ellen finds them a bit right-wing.'

'And what do you know about it?' she replied. 'Talk about political illiteracy!'

I finished the coffee and stood up to go.

'Are you coming to the party?' Mark asked.

'I don't think so.'

'You should come, man. We're playing. It's for Frelimo.'

'Who's Frelimo?'

'It's the Mozambique Liberation Front,' explained Ellen. 'We're doing a party tomorrow in aid of the Committee for Freedom in Angola, Mozambique and Guinea.'

'All right, I'll come. I'll see you tomorrow then,' I said, waving vaguely at the group from the door.

'Far out man,' said Mark.

'Peace,' said Luke, without opening his eyes.

By the following morning I had decided that the last thing I wanted to do was to go to the Frelimo party. Then Ellen left a note in my pigeonhole saying she would come to fetch me and I changed my mind. The note also suggested I might wear more comfortable clothes.

She arrived in my rooms wearing a silk scarf around her forehead and an enormous sheepskin coat she had bought in Afghanistan.

'You look almost normal in jeans,' she told me.

'They're my only pair and I've never worn them at Oxford. Would you like a glass of sherry?'

'I don't drink.'

'But you smoke.'

'Certain substances. Don't you?'

'Never.' I smiled. 'I suppose one day we might discover something we have in common.'

'I think we might.'

She was going through my books, running her fore-finger along the tops.

'Perhaps we have already,' she remarked. 'Zola, for example, and George Eliot. Not bad. I didn't expect them.' She went on looking and finally said, 'And the only book I was sure I would find isn't here.'

'Which was that?'

'*Brideshead Revisited*.'

'You consider that a good sign?'

'Very good.'

'I'm afraid my well-thumbed copy has been borrowed.'

I invited her to eat something and suggested we went to the Cantina.

'Fine, but how do we get from there to the party?'

'I have a car. Don't worry – it's a Ford not a Rolls Royce.'

We wrapped up and walked out through the two quads. By the porter's lodge we passed Haldane. He looked at me, then at Ellen, said 'Good God!' loudly and walked on.

'I guess you found those guys kind of weird,' Ellen said as we chewed our way through a plate of pasta.

'Well, I've never come face to face with flower power before.'

'And I've never met anyone who has led such a cocooned existence as you.'

But she did not say it aggressively. There was no more

talk about the eighteenth century and *droit de seigneur*. I think we both found it strange that we could talk easily after that unpromising first meeting.

'Is one of them your boy friend?' I asked.

'Not really. I mean I sleep with Mark sometimes, but you couldn't call it a love affair. I don't get jealous if he makes it with someone else.'

I was surprised by a sudden feeling of annoyance. I wasn't yet sure that I liked Ellen Hartman, but she was intelligent and self-possessed and there was a pinched haunting beauty about her face. At any rate she seemed much too good for a dim guitarist with greasy hair.

During dinner she told me about her life. She was not, as I had imagined, a rebel striking back at a comfortable middle-class life in Brooklyn. The rebels had been her parents – a Jewish father and a southern Baptist mother who had joined the Communist Party as teenagers.

'My dad fought in Spain with the Lincoln Brigade. He got wounded at Jarama and was taken home. Do you know the song?'

She hummed a couple of bars and then crooned the lines:

> 'There's a valley in Spain called Jarama,
> It's a place that we all know so well.
> It was there that we gave of our manhood,
> Where so many of our brave comrades fell.

I'll play it to you on the guitar some day.'

Her parents had naturally suffered in the McCarthy era. Her father had been arraigned for 'unAmerican activities' and could find only ill-paid work in radical journalism; her mother had had a modest success as a sculptress. But the family was not poor. Financial help had come from her uncles, who were New York dentists,

74

and Ellen had been able to study at Berkeley. Most of her views, it seemed, were extensions of her parents' politics adapted for a different generation. Instead of the fight against fascism and the Nazis, it was the struggle against imperialism in the Third World; instead of Abyssinia it was Vietnam; instead of Hitler and Mussolini it was Vorster and Lyndon B. Johnson. The civil and feminist issues remained much the same though they had been extended to include the legalization of cannabis and abortion. Ellen admitted that there had been a change of emphasis. The Thirties had promoted armed struggle as the panacea for everything; in the Sixties you preached peace to make the West withdraw. Ellen was a Marxist who belonged to no party, though she was close to both the Socialist Workers and the International Marxists. She had an instinctive sympathy with all anti-Western liberation movements and most totalitarian groups of the Left. But she was also a hippie, dabbling in Indian mysticism and distrusting all governments, who had not yet resolved the contradictions of her mixed beliefs.

I was glad we had gone to the restaurant because at the party it was impossible to talk. The noise was terrible and seemed to bear no relation to music or to musical instruments: it was just a booming of the drums and the bass guitar and a screeching of everything else. A girl by the door, who was handing out Frelimo badges, said something to me which I didn't hear. I decided I couldn't spend the whole evening saying 'what?' or 'sorry?' so I just grinned at her. A huge black man in a cowboy hat enveloped Ellen in his arms and wouldn't let her go. I wondered irritably whether he was another lover and then wondered how many people in the room she might have slept with.

Eventually he released her and she grabbed my hand and pulled me through a jostling crowd of orange clothes and frizzy Afro hairstyles. Other people greeted her and I merely stood behind and grinned; I would have felt more self-conscious without the Cantina's wine in my stomach. Eventually we reached the room where people were dancing. Strobe lighting flickered across the floor, giving an impression that the dancers were suffering from demonic convulsions. Many of them were gyrating by themselves with their eyes shut, experiencing some private ecstasy. On a stage at the far end of the hall was the band. Gwendolen was singing but it was impossible to make out what the song was about or even if it had words. Boris was bashing any drum or cymbal within range while Mark leapt about the stage holding his guitar as if it were alternately a machine-gun or a hobby-horse. Behind them Luke was playing bass; he was at least standing up but his eyes were serenely closed.

The large black man had reappeared and I thought of leaving. There was no obligation to stay because Mark would presumably be taking Ellen back. I looked again at him. One couldn't blame him for sweating so much during his lunatic performance, but all the same no one could deny that he looked repellent, jumping around and behaving as if he were having an orgasm with his guitar. Ellen touched me on the shoulder and suggested we went outside.

In the hallway we collected our coats and she introduced me to the black man and a girl called Rita.

'Morgan's got some pot,' she said.

'It's great, man,' said Morgan. 'Straight from Kathmandu.'

'You want to try some?' she asked quietly, so that the others would not realize I was a hash novice.

All right, I thought, let's crowd in the new experiences. We went to Morgan's van and he and Rita sat in the front mixing the cannabis with tobacco and rolling the stuff in a cigarette paper. He lit the end, inhaled and passed it to

Ellen. She drew lightly, held the breath in her lungs and then let the smoke out gently through her nostrils.

'Man, that's a great joint,' she said, handing it to me.

'What did I tell you babe?' said Morgan. 'Turn right on.'

The smoke was so bitter and acrid that I instantly choked. I tried again, with more success, and gave it to Rita.

'You smuggled this stuff all the way from Nepal?' I asked.

'No man, I scored in Piccadilly Circus, right beside Eros. But I know the cat who sold it to me and he never tells lies.'

We finished the joint and all I had was a nasty taste in my mouth. When Morgan rolled another, I inhaled deeply, determined to experience some sensation. It was probably during the third joint that I began to feel curiously light-headed and detached. I looked at my hands and thought they were no longer mine because they could function by themselves. My head seemed weightless and I felt I was almost floating. Rita said something I didn't understand and I think I said 'peace'. I noticed they were all laughing at me.

'Man, are you spaced out!' said Morgan.

'Why are you laughing?' I asked Ellen.

'Because you're so cute,' she said, leaning over to give me a light kiss. When she sat up, I pulled her back and forced her head above mine. Her hair was over my face and in my eyes, but I found her mouth and kissed her and she didn't resist. I heard Morgan say, 'Ellen, where did you find this crazy man?' but she didn't answer. We went on kissing for what seemed an age and finally she stopped and said we must be going.

I staggered out of the van into the freezing night and had to crouch down suddenly to prevent myself fainting.

'I think I'd better drive,' said Ellen.

Perhaps I would have killed us if I had driven, but Ellen nearly killed us anyway. She misjudged a bend in the road and the car skidded on the ice, hitting a wall and then a lamp-post before coming to a halt on the pavement. The engine stopped and there was an absolute silence.

'Jesus!' she exclaimed, 'are you all right?'

My side of the car had crashed into the post and something had hit me on the head.

'I think so.'

I couldn't recognize where we were, but it must have been an area of offices or laboratories. No one was around and nobody came out of the buildings to see what had happened.

'We'd better split before the fuzz come.'

'What?'

'The police,' Ellen explained.

I suddenly realized that blood was surging from my forehead. It was in my hair and on my lips and dripping on to my jeans.

'I think I've taken a bit of a knock.'

'My God, it's all over you.' She took the scarf off her head. 'Put that against the wound and hold it tight. I'm going to take you to the Infirmary.'

She managed to get the car re-started and drove slowly off. I noticed the lamp-post was badly bent but I can recall little else about that night. The Radcliffe seemed all lights and stretchers and nurses peering at my head. I remember Ellen's American voice calmly explaining how the incident happened, then X-rays and an injection and a line of stitches along the top of my forehead. I must have been there for a couple of hours before I heard a doctor talking to Ellen.

'You can take him home now. But look after him.'

It was four in the morning when a minicab took us to

78

my college. Ellen led me in, my head covered in bandages, and explained to the inquisitive porter what had happened. In my rooms she found honey and lemon and made some hot drinks.

'How do you feel now?'

'A bit peculiar. I don't know if it's the cannabis or the accident or just shock.'

'It's probably all of them.'

She helped me undress and wash, scrubbing the dried blood from the back of my neck. It didn't seem odd that I should be standing there almost naked with a strange girl ministering to me. I felt it was the sort of camaraderie one might experience after a battle. She found my pyjamas and I put them on while she turned down the bed. Then she disappeared into the sitting room and came back with an armful of cushions.

'What are you doing?'

She laid the cushions in a line on the floor.

'I'm going to sleep here,' she smiled, 'in case you get nightmares.'

I lay down and she knelt beside the bed and took my hand.

'Jesus, I'm sorry.'

'There's no need to be.'

'But I am.'

She bent over and kissed me, and I could feel she was giggling.

'What are you laughing about now?'

'Just a funny thought.'

'What?'

'I was wondering,' she mused, 'how I'm going to explain all this to Janet Black.'

The following October, at the beginning of our final year, Ellen and I rented a flat west of the Infirmary in Jericho. Few undergraduates lived there, but we didn't mind because we needed to work. I had eight months before history finals; Ellen, two years older than me, was writing her thesis on the East End opposition to Mosley's black-shirts. It was a good period, of work and calm and each other's company, of occasional evenings with other students and music. The pop group had departed for the United States and her other friends were very different from Boris and Mark. They were serious people who read Sartre and Marcuse, took part in political demonstrations and contrived to admire Mao's China and hippie liber-tarianism at the same time.

Our most surprising visitor that autumn was Haldane. I watched as he drove up one evening, slamming the car door and scowling at the terrace of redbrick houses.

'What a ghastly area,' he said gruffly as he entered the sitting room. 'Why the hell do you live here? What's the point of being at Oxford if you live in a part that looks like Darlington?'

Haldane had rooms in Merton Street, in the house of his father's old landlady.

'What's wrong with Darlington?' asked Ellen as she went to make some coffee.

'Everything.'

'Have you been there?'

'I've been through it. You can tell exactly what it's like from the train. All bricks and pigeon fanciers.'

Haldane was in the middle of his term as president of the Union, a post he had won at the second attempt in the summer. He had arranged a debate on the Vietnam war for that Thursday and he needed advice. One of the anti-American speakers had cancelled and he wondered whether Ellen could suggest a replacement.

'I thought you might know how to get hold of Danny the Red or some other revo. I imagine they're friends of yours.'

Ellen gave him some names and offered him more coffee. Haldane said, 'I know this is a pacifist vegetarian commune and all that, but is it teetotal as well? I mean, is there any chance of a whisky and soda?'

We had some wine and Haldane settled for that, although he looked at the bottle for a bit and said the Yugoslavs should be banned from exporting their riesling. He drank half the bottle and then turned on Ellen with the half-querulous, half-jesting tone typical of him.

'I don't know what you've done to bewitch my friend Gordon. He used to be quite sensible. Sound views on most things, except field sports of course. Could lower port with the best of us. And now look. He's been corrupted by you and gone completely off the rails.'

'The guy's just seen the light,' said Ellen.

'Hallucinations,' said Haldane and muttered something provocative about 'Americans meddling with the aristocracy'.

I knew he was telling people both in Oxford and Scotland that Hugh Gordon was a lost cause, a decent chap who had been brainwashed by a harridan from Brooklyn. But I didn't mind. It was obvious that Ellen had influenced me, yet she didn't impose her views and I often disagreed with her. I did move to the Left, accepting the premises of social democracy and opposing the American intervention in south-east Asia. I agreed with the basic platform of the women's movement and took the liberal side on abortion and homosexuality – though on none of these issues did I go so far as Ellen. But I rejected Marxist views of history and I did not think

81

totalitarian régimes of the Left preferable to authoritarian régimes of the Right. I could not become enthusiastic about all her causes. Ellen had wanted to go to Paris the previous May to show solidarity with the students; but to me they seemed middle-class youths playing at revolution, and the Communist Party seemed right not to jeopardize its future for the sake of their egotism.

After meeting Ellen I began to look at things in different ways. She was justified in complaining about my cocooned childhood, for I had had little experience of anything. The only poor people I had ever known were the widows of estate workers who were always well provided for; they lived in neat cottages with dahlias and hollyhocks in the front garden, and they always smiled when they saw my grandparents. In the Lothian mining towns I had noticed women and children who seemed poorer, but I saw them only through a car window and never went inside their homes. Communism and capitalism produced their distinctive brands of misery and I disliked them both. Was there anything better, I sometimes wondered, than an ordered rural society, everyone with his own place in the community, everyone with an individual role to play? There was slavery and anonymity in the mines and the textile mills but not in the rural parish. And if every form of society needed a head, wasn't a philanthropic squire preferable to a Getty or a commissar?

But with Ellen you were always aware of the bad squires, the greedy and the lecherous, the landlords who despised and exploited their labourers. I abandoned them without regret. It was a relief to be with people who neither knew nor cared that I was the heir of Starne, a future earl, 'scion' – as I was so often boringly reminded – 'of an ancient line'. There was much to be said for the anonymity and universalism of the hippie generation where backgrounds and accents did not matter. I was happy to lose myself in that stateless and classless Anglo-American brotherhood, happy to belong to a culture which seemed to have an irrefutable message of its own. Of course there were conventions, even a uniformity, about our unconventional behaviour. We spoke much the same language, smoked the same cannabis, wore the same type of waistcoats from Herat. We bought the same Bob Dylan records (there was some poetry in him after all) and read the same books: Hesse and Gibran and Simone de Beauvoir, but never Hemingway or Evelyn Waugh. Yet there was something reassuring about this conformity: it expressed an identity as well as solidarity in the struggle against the materialist and the reactionary.

When our Oxford years ended, Ellen and I travelled for a few months in southern Africa. We went to Rhodesia and the Portuguese colonies and visited the Frelimo leaders in Dar es Salaam. After Ellen was expelled from South Africa for writing an article about the Bantustans, we returned to London and settled in a flat in Earls Court. I worked as an editor for a publisher producing a series of books on Africa and the Third World. Ellen accumulated a mass of different tasks, giving lectures and radio broadcasts, organizing seminars, hammering out polemical articles on her typewriter. A single day might be divided between a meeting of the Greek Committee against Dictatorship, a talk at the LSE and a spell on the picket outside South Africa House. Demonstrations took up a lot of her time and I often went with her; it was exhilarating protesting with the crowds outside the American embassy against the Vietnam war.

Sometimes we went to rock concerts or festivals; in the summer of '71 we travelled to the Isle of Wight and camped for three days to see Dylan. But politics had now become an obsession for Ellen and she had little time for music. She had become a collector of causes which stretched all around the world, causes which were always black and white: one side was always right and the aggressor was always the West.

We had been in London for nearly three years when Ellen discovered she was pregnant. I was surprised because she was efficient in nearly all things.

'It was a mistake?'

'Yes.'

'You know I'll make any arrangements you want.'

'I don't know. I'm thinking of keeping the baby.'

'And give up your work?'

'Only for a time. I could do most of the things again afterwards.'

She came up to my desk chair and put her hands on my shoulders.

'Wouldn't you like me to have your baby?'

She emphasized lightly the penultimate word so as to avoid an unnecessary question.

'If you want it, then I want it too.'

She leant back against the table and put her hands on her stomach.

'I know it's crazy, I've never wanted one before, but now that it's there . . . I think I must have it.'

Later I asked if she wanted to get married. She shrugged her shoulders.

'I'm not bothered. It makes no difference to me.'

'Rightly or wrongly, it would make a difference to the child. And perhaps also to me.'

She sighed. 'I'm not sure. I don't want to be tied down.'

'You won't be. It'll be a formality.'

'You understand that I wouldn't change, don't you? I wouldn't become Lady Starne or whatever when your father dies.'

'Of course not. It will all be the same. With the same rules,' I added.

The rules were negative and unspoken: no questions, no lies and no confessions. You had to tell the truth but not all of the truth. We lived together because we wanted to, without any sense of obligation; if either of us had wanted a serious relationship with someone else, we would have separated. But as for casual affairs, a night at a UNA conference, an idle afternoon at a friend's flat, they were different and did not matter. Nevertheless, we had a pact that we didn't ask questions: we knew that confessed infidelity, however unimportant and fleeting for the participant, could cause irrational and disproportionate hurt for the other.

We were married on an April afternoon at the local registry office. A week later, while her pregnancy was still invisible, I took Ellen north to meet my father.

iv

My grandparents had died during the first half of my time at Oxford. They had gone within a year of each other and people said they had died well, as they had lived and as they would have wished. Certainly there had been no problems with senility or long illness, but I doubted whether my grandmother would have chosen to fall from the cliffs at St Abb's Head while looking at seabirds.

She had often told us she did not want to be buried in case she was dug up, like her sister, by thieves looking for jewellery. (We thought her own rings had been stolen until they were found, long after her death, in her hot-water bottle.) She also told us she didn't want to be a bore when dead so the easiest thing would be simply to fling her ashes from the top of some hill. However, a late codicil to her will contained a more fanciful instruction: her ashes were to be thrown from the Dean Bridge in Edinburgh and the water would carry them down to Leith, where she had done much charity work between the wars. Perhaps she had forgotten how high the bridge stood above the river, for even on a still day it would have required luck and a good aim to guide the ashes into the narrow Water of Leith. Perhaps also she had failed to picture the absurdity of the scene, the small group of mourners standing on the slender pavement while amazed motorists sped past. Anyway, the little ceremony was not a success. As my father tipped the urn's contents over the high parapet, a gust of wind blew up from the north and scattered the ashes over the onlookers.

After his wife's death my grandfather tried to be cheerful; he drank more port and told more stories. But it was clear he had been much affected and his physical decline accelerated. He could walk less far and shoot less well, so that to many people it seemed a relief when he died the next summer at his beloved Ravensmuir. It happened after lunch on the moors. He simply walked up to his place, laid his gun in the heather and leant back against the butt for a short nap; he never woke up.

'What a fine way to go,' people told me afterwards, 'wish I could go like that.' We buried him in the ruined abbey at Starne and afterwards we gave a lunch for his friends. They allotted epitaphs of an appropriately sporting character. 'He had a good innings,' they said; 'He died as he had lived, in the saddle.' Doubtless they were right to say it was better to die like that, suddenly, instead of going downhill for years. But for me both deaths were desolating. They were the deaths of people I had known and loved all my life, since I was aware of anything, and they seemed more shattering, more of a convulsion, than the death of a close but recent friend. I felt as if my childhood had followed my grandfather's body into that roofless chapel.

Since then my father had divided his year almost evenly between Starne and his panelled rooms in Cambridge. He remained a don at Trinity and still taught during the term, but in the vacations he brought his books and papers to Scotland. His divorced sister Pamela usually accompanied him but without her daughters; Beatrice had gone to Canada and Clarissa was studying in Florence. My aunt tried to organize his life at Starne and was often exhorting him (and myself as well in frequent unsought letters) to take more interest in the estate. 'The whole place will go to the dogs,' she wrote, 'unless someone takes a firm hand now.' She was insistent that my father sack Logan, whom she accused of being a useless factor, and Machale who, she claimed, had drunk his way through half the cellar. 'One should never have a guardsman as a butler,' she declared. 'They tyrannize the staff and drink all the Chambertin.'

My father did not sack them. Nor did he pay much attention to her other suggestions. There was no need, he thought, to install modern bathrooms or replace the massive iron radiators; apart from anything else, no one was going to use them. And he saw no need to fill the house with art experts and valuers; if he wasn't going to sell his pictures, he said, he did not need to know how much they were worth. Only when something critical occurred, such as an outbreak of dry rot in the west wing, did he sanction expensive alterations. Only when he had to make a drastic decision, such as the sale of the Ravensmuir estate after the fire, did he telephone me to discuss it.

'I know you like the place,' he had said drily, a few days after the lodge had burnt to the ground, 'but it's not much use to us. Neither of us shoots and we can't afford to rebuild it. Besides, I've got these infernal taxes to pay.'

The changes at Starne after my grandfather's death were so subtle and personal that they were hardly noticeable. An elephant's foot, used as an umbrella stand in the outer hall, was thrown out. The flag was no longer flown from the tower when the laird was at home. My grandfather's collections of 'Jorrocks' and other hunting stories were removed from the library and replaced by old editions of Virgil and Ovid. And in the cloakroom a framed copy of Kipling's 'If' was taken down and expelled. Ornately decorated in imitation of a medieval manuscript, it had hung there, above the loo, ever since I could remember. I had learnt the poem unwittingly at an early age and I had been struck by certain lines:

If you can dream – and not make dreams your master,
If you can think – and not make thoughts your aim;
If you can meet with Triumph and Disaster
And treat those two impostors just the same.

When I noticed it was no longer there, I wondered unkindly if my father had removed it because he had failed the test set by those last two lines. But later I realized I was wrong, for even in triumph he had hated Kipling.

My father's book on the Greeks of Syracuse had been published after eight years of research and writing. Although it sold few copies, it was a critical success, reviewers placing him in the same league as Moses Finley and the other Hellenists of his generation. But since then he had produced no major work. There was talk of a book on Magna Graecia and a history of the Greeks in the central Mediterranean, works which would have consolidated his reputation. But they did not materialize. He turned to writing essays on recondite subjects which he produced very slowly. Annually a solitary article used to appear in some academic journal: 'On the theory of Ostracism', 'In defence of Oligarchy', a piece on the Stoics, a long and inconclusive disquisition on whether the *Iliad* and the *Odyssey* had been written by the same person. Eventually they were collected and published in one volume, but few publications reviewed it.

So academic disappointment was ultimately added to the failures of his marriage and his political career. And, like the earlier defeats, he reacted to it by a further withdrawal from the society of other people. I think he had one or two friends among the dons at Cambridge, but in Scotland he rarely saw anyone. He went to Edinburgh only if he had to meet his lawyers or if he needed to look up something in the library. He never went to the New Club after its Georgian premises in Princes Street had been pulled down, and he no longer went to concerts. Any pleasure gained from the music, he insisted, was invariably outweighed by his irritation with the audience: he was infuriated by people who coughed or rustled papers or leant forward and obscured the view.

His crustiness seemed to have become more truculent when I took Ellen to visit him at Starne. He had expressed neither pleasure nor interest in the news of my marriage, and he appeared to regard our visit as a tiresome interruption of his solitude. No effort was made to welcome us and no car was sent to the station. Although there were flowers in our room and wine at meals, I was sure they had been produced on the telephoned instructions of Aunt Pamela.

On that first evening, while we sat awkwardly in the library, my father recounted a series of petty triumphs in which he had snubbed recent intruders.

'Some damned journalist rang this morning to ask if

it's true we have a hundred and twenty rooms. How should I know? I told him I wasn't going to go round counting them and put the telephone down.'

'Would you like me to count them,' asked Ellen with a smile, 'in case it happens again?'

Her accent appeared to remind him of another well-administered rebuff.

'You will hardly credit this,' he said, 'but I found an American in the hall last week. An ordinary American, a tourist, wandering about with cameras inside a private house. He inquired if he might see anything of the building, so I said stonily, "By all means. You may start with the front door – from the outside." You should have seen his astonishment. It was most amusing.'

At dinner he was in a better humour, but the wine which seemed to mollify him had the opposite effect on Ellen. She seldom drank and had the lightest of heads; it needed only a glass or two to make her politically combative. Yet she began harmlessly, asking my father questions about Scotland which he answered courteously. It was only after several minutes that I realized she had somehow acquired muddled and naive ideas about Scottish nationalism. Scotland was a nation, she appeared to believe, which had been conquered and exploited by England and was now justifiably demanding its independence. She even talked about 'the national struggle' as if Scotland were a Third World colony and the SNP a liberation movement like Frelimo.

'But they've been fighting for centuries for their independence,' she claimed.

'They fought several hundred years ago, not in recent centuries.'

'What about those Jacobite people?'

'The Jacobites aspired to change the king in London. They were not Scottish nationalists and in 1745 they did not have the support of a single great chieftain in the Highlands.'

'Well, every country has its quislings and Uncle Toms . . .'

'More Scots, dear girl, fought for the Hanoverians than for the Jacobite side.'

'But not the patriots.'

'They all considered themselves equally patriotic. I refer, of course, to the small minority on either side that understood the concept.'

I tried to intervene but it was no use. I had seen Ellen in action like this many times before, normally in committee meetings, and she never backed down. Yet she was usually more knowledgeable about her subject and she seldom had to argue with people as percipient as my father.

'Scotland became a wealthy country in the eighteenth century,' he stated, 'following the union with England. It owed everything to the union, its industry, its Enlightenment, its role in the empire.'

'Nevertheless, it was exploited.'

'By whom?'

'The English, the landlords who expropriated the Highlands and expelled the people because they could make more money with sheep.'

'The landlords, dear girl, were Scottish.'

'Well, it's normal in backward societies for feudal leaders to ally themselves with the colonialist power against the masses. Anyway, you can't deny that the Highlanders were expelled.'

'Most of them were not expelled. The great majority left because they did not want to starve. Furthermore, at the end of the so-called Clearances there were more people living in the Highlands than at the beginning.'

My father was plainly enjoying himself. He had

probably not had such an easy target for years, his undergraduate pupils being unlikely to expose themselves as recklessly as Ellen. It was easy to imagine his sarcasm if a student had dared compare modern imperialism with Athens and the Delian League.

He walked over to the sideboard and searched among the half-empty bottles.

'Here we are,' he said, waving one of them. 'I was sure we had some ancient Armagnac.' He returned with the bottle, smiling in anticipation of a new round.

Ellen unwisely accepted a glass and then suggested that the 'real' Scotland was Celtic and therefore the revival of Gaelic should be promoted. My father replied that the real Scotland had been Anglo-Norman since at least the twelfth century and that Gaelic was a useless language incapable of modern adaptation. Like Welsh and Basque, he added.

'Moreover,' he continued, 'if you want to go back a thousand years to the Gaelic-speaking Scots, why not go back a bit further to the Gaelic-speaking Picts? They were the indigenous inhabitants of the land because, as I'm sure you are aware, the Scots came from Ireland. Unfortunately,' he remarked, 'the Picts are no longer with us. In that respect they resemble the Red Indians.'

The conversation then jumped forward a few centuries and ended with Ellen demanding to know if my father denied the Scots the right to elect their own assembly.

'A Scottish assembly!' he exclaimed. 'My dear girl, what nonsense. Instead of having our councillors misruling Lothian, we should have them misgoverning the whole of Scotland. We would be displaying to the world our present mean and narrow-minded provincialism.'

The following morning I wanted to show Ellen the house and the policies, but it was hardly worth going outside. One of the county's famous mists had descended, surrounding the house and obscuring the views of the sea and the hills; the boundaries of visibility extended only as far as the looming elms in the park.

Ellen did not greatly admire the house. Perhaps she was feeling tired after the unaccustomed wine and the Armagnac; perhaps her baby made her feel sick; or perhaps she was simply annoyed by my father and by her own performance the night before. She was, for whatever reason, in an unappreciative mood.

'But why did they need so many rooms? What did they do in them? What was the point of having a red drawing room and a green drawing room? They needed to take a rest from the colours?'

She wanted to meet people – the cook, the gardener, some farmworkers – presumably to see how downtrodden and exploited they were. But she found it difficult to talk to them, her efforts usually ending with them shaking their heads and saying, 'Och, it's miserable weather.'

We stayed only three days and on our last evening the mist lifted and a watery sunset covered the landscape in a gentle roseate light. I could see it heralded the typical late spring of the east coast when there is no visible movement until the middle of April and then a week of warm weather brings everything out in a rush. I knew that within a few days the primroses and the wild garlic would be out, the chestnut leaves would be hanging in clusters, and the pale greens of the beech and the young birch would appear; then, almost overnight, the dead grass stems and the bare hawthorn would dissolve in a burst of bright green and the last of winter would have gone.

I tried to explain this to Ellen and tell her how beautiful it would be. But it was too late. She found the place oppressive, with the weather, my father and the hundred and twenty rooms, and she was unable to see good in it. That evening she argued for the last time with her father-in-law.

'The essential difference between your generation and ours,' she told him, 'is that yours lacked compassion.'

'You are referring to the generation that was killed in the war?'

'No, I'm not referring to the dead guys but to everybody who caused and fought the war, everybody who got us into that mess because they were concerned only with national interests.'

'The essential difference between your generation and mine,' he replied quietly, '– indeed the essential difference between yours and the four or five preceding ones – is that we had, or felt we had, a duty, and you don't. It may have been a mistaken one, though I think not, but it gave us a purpose in life. You talk a good deal about fascism but I spent five years of my life fighting it, in North Africa and Italy. My brother was killed at Alamein and I watched him die. My father fought throughout the previous war and his brother was also killed, on the Western Front, with the best of his generation. Our grandfathers and their fathers struggled too for what they believed, in Africa or India or here at home. A hundred years later it's easy to scoff at the missionaries and the civil servants who gave their lives for the people of the tropics. But what do you think people will be saying, a century from now, of the generation which tried to install Marxism in the jungle?'

My father closed his eyes and even Ellen seemed subdued briefly by his eloquence. I looked at him and at last I understood why he hated our pampered and self-indulgent generation. I understood why someone who had been through Anzio and Alamein should have such resentment for our ignorant self-assurance. I thought of the trenches and my dead uncles and the millions of other corpses, and I paid little attention to an argument Ellen had begun about jobs and the dole. Then suddenly I heard her say in her quiet, knowing, irritating way, 'There's no unemployment in the Soviet Union,' and I put my hands over my eyes and thought, 'Oh God, why doesn't she stop? How can she go on saying such stupid things?'

'No,' said my father gently, 'I expect not. Nor was there unemployment among the slaves in the American plantations. Nor among the helots of Sparta. Nor in any society where the labour force is treated as slaves.'

He shook his head and poured the last drops of the Armagnac into his glass.

'You remind me, my dear, of a very clever gentleman called Plato who lived nearly two and a half thousand years ago. He was a native of Athens, the most democratic and civilized state of his time, perhaps of all time. But he hated Athens and admired its great enemy Sparta, a totalitarian state barren of cultural life. And he praised that frightful place, ignoring the fact that if he had lived there he would have enjoyed none of the culture or freedom that enabled him to live and teach and write in Athens. When I hear intelligent people in the West praising Russia, I generally think of Plato.'

v

During the remaining half-decade of my father's life, I visited him twice a year alone. He always made an enquiry about Ellen's health but never spoke of her otherwise. When Lucy was born he said, 'Mother and child doing well I trust?', but on Stephen's birth two years later he merely grunted, 'So this gloomy place will have an heir after all.' He never indicated a desire to see his grand-children.

I travelled to Starne a week after he had returned from his last journey abroad.

'I went to Syracuse,' he reported, 'for the first time in seventeen years. I shall never go back, neither to Sicily nor to the rest of Europe. It is of an unimaginable horror.'

Wiping his spectacles at the breakfast table, he looked querulously at me.

'It was a great error to return and lose my last illusions. I cannot conceive how they could have destroyed that matchless bay at Augusta – why couldn't they have put their hideous refineries elsewhere? And then you come to Syracuse, your head full of Aeschylus and Simonides. But it's useless even to try to imagine them as you travel through those dismal outskirts: green blocks of flats, then mauve ones and finally orange. At last you reach the Greek remains. But they too have lost their magic. Heavy lorries thunder past the Neapolis and American tourists besiege the Ear of Dionysius. It was unspeakable!'

There was enough to annoy him in Britain too, an accumulation of vexations which impelled him to write weekly letters of complaint to *The Times* and the *Scotsman*. He behaved as if there were a conspiracy to irritate old people by changing things that did not need to be changed. Wherever possible he stuck to the old usages. He refused to recognize the new regional boundaries, continuing to address his letters as if the old counties still existed. He talked about the Third Programme and the Home Service, never referring to them by their new names. And he made a stand against decimal coinage by continuing to add a 'd' to denote the number of pence on his cheques. This particular protest ended in humiliation.

'Do you know what that idiot clerk in Haddington did? He handed my cheque back with the words, "It's pence sir, not dence".'

In his middle sixties my father seemed older than my grandfather had done in his middle seventies. But it was not only the fastidious irascibility which contributed to the impression of age. He was in poor health although he denied it and refused to see a doctor. He said he had a smoker's cough, caused by four decades of pipe tobacco, but when I heard the outbursts of coughing in his study, I knew it was something more serious.

'The doctor thinks it's emphysema,' said Aunt Pamela. 'I managed to deceive your father into thinking he had come to see me, so he was able to have a quick inspection.'

To counter the irritations of the present, my father lived increasingly in the past. He was aided by a memory that forgot what he had done yesterday but retained conversations of fifty years before. He had rarely spoken to me of his childhood but now his conversation consisted largely of reminiscence. I remember his telling me that the saddest moment of his early life had been the transformation of the stables for motor cars; he had watched the joiners tearing out the loose-boxes and removing his donkey cart from its accustomed place.

He listened to the past as well, and not merely to the timeless past of his favourite composer Bach, but to the popular music of his youth, to records of Vera Lynn or Flanagan and Allen; sometimes I heard him humming 'Underneath the Arches' along the corridor. He also acquired a transistor radio, or wireless as he called it, which he carried around with him. It was curious to pass the muniment room, where he spent much of his time looking at old documents, and hear Roy Plomley and his guest on *Desert Island Discs*. After my father's death I found among his papers a short list of pieces of music. It puzzled me for a while until suddenly I understood its significance: it listed the records he would have chosen had he been invited to appear on Plomley's programme.

I also found a number of unfinished essays, none of them in his own academic field, which he had worked on intermittently during those last years. There were a few pages discussing the authorship of the 'Canadian Boating Song' and a longer piece on 'tragedy and the River Yarrow' in the Border ballads. A third was entitled 'Progress to What?' and was followed by a quotation from Disraeli's *Tancred*.

And yet some flat-nosed Frank, full of bustle and puffed up with self-conceit . . . talks of Progress! Progress to what, and from where? Amid empires shrivelled into deserts, amid the wrecks of great cities, a single column or obelisk of which nations import for the prime ornament of their mud-built capitals, amid arts forgotten, commerce annihilated, fragmentary literatures, and populations destroyed, the European talks of progress, because by an ingenious application of some scientific acquirements, he has established a society which has mistaken comfort for civilization.

The illusion of 'progress' was the last obsession of my father's life, an obsession that was a suitable climax to a lifetime of pessimistic thought. I became aware of it during an evening's walk at Starne in his penultimate summer. It had been a grey dreary afternoon but after tea the clouds had lifted and the late sun had caught the Isle of May and the blue waters of the Forth. Between the elms of the park we could see the Bass Rock lit up with a warm incarnadine glow as if reflecting the light of a great fire miles away.

'Look at that sky,' my father said suddenly, pointing upwards with his stick. 'It's wonderful and yet we don't appreciate it.' The heavens were soft and lightly streaked with pink, the clouds looking as if they were feathered, interwoven in a single design resembling the shape of a gigantic angel's wing.

'Why don't we admire the sky's beauty,' he said quietly, 'as we ought to? Is it because we have not yet spoilt it? Do you think we love beautiful things only when they are threatened?'

We strolled past the loch and down through the old alder wood.

'Were these trees planted?' I asked.

'Yes, they were once thought quite valuable. There was a proverb which went something like "the alder will buy the horse before the oak buys the saddle". Probably all nonsense.'

In a clearing at the bottom of the hill we came across a timber haulage lorry belonging to contractors hired by Logan. It was stacked with grey beech trunks trussed together like great carcasses after the slaughter house.

'Shouldn't we be planting more trees?' I asked.

'I doubt there's much point,' replied my father gloomily. 'Those were planted by our ancestors in the belief that they would have two hundred years to develop before being cut down by their descendants. How can we, in this appalling age, plan ahead for centuries? We don't know if we'll be here for two years, let alone two hundred. It's a waste of time for people to plant trees nowadays. Either they'll be cut down to make way for roads and bungalows, or else they'll be poisoned by the atmosphere.'

Around that time I noticed he had abandoned his journals on classical studies which he used to read in the evenings. He now bought magazines on nature and the environment and cut out articles that might be useful for his essay 'Progress to What?' Statistics of endangered species and disappearing flora were copied out and repeated to anyone he saw. 'Did you realize,' he might ask me or Machale or the postmistress in the village, 'that we have destroyed ninety per cent of our water meadows since the Second World War?' My father supported his new cause with donations. A large number of cheques, our accountant felt obliged to warn me, were being sent each week to save creatures such as pilot whales or the gorillas of Rwanda.

There was nothing left worth doing, my father believed, except to preserve things. If he was young again, he assured me, he would be a conservationist or a game warden in Africa. 'But even that is too late. They can only delay things, throwing sand against the wind. They cannot reverse the tide of self-destruction. Good God! We're worse than lemmings, we've become like the Gadarene swine!'

We were sitting by the library fireplace on an autumn evening when you could hear the gales coming down the chimneys. The previous year some old trees had been cut down in the orchard and the bitter-sweet smell of cherry wood now wafted from the fire. My father was almost lying in his armchair, his feet in old leather slippers stretched out towards the hearth, his left hand rubbing his forehead as if gently trying to erase the lines of old age.

'I used to think of the world improving slowly over the millennia since the Sumerians built the first civilization. There were advances and setbacks but still we seemed to inch forward until we came to the monsters of our own time. I thought we had been pushing a rock uphill for centuries but I was wrong. It's coming downhill fast – what we call Progress or Civilization but what is in reality self-destruction. It's landing on top of us, devouring everything it can see – nature, the animal kingdom, the weaker human societies – and eventually it will devour us, its greedy begetters, as well.'

He paused to cough and then looked at the fire, shaking his grey head.

'How could intelligent people, men who were pioneers of science and biology, who measured gradual evolution over millions of years – how could they not have understood that a brief period of massive industrialization would end with the destruction of the world?'

It was not until a few weeks before his death that my father admitted he was ill. He knew it was not emphysema: indeed, I believe he had known months earlier that he was going to die of lung cancer and had decided not to resist it. We forced him to go to Edinburgh for an intensive course of radiation therapy, but the disease was too advanced for any treatment; it had already spread to his oesophagus and adrenal glands. When they realized this, the doctors did not attempt to conceal the truth or to persuade him to stay in hospital.

'I have only a few days left,' he announced, his eyes closed in visible pain, 'and I wish to spend them in my home.'

So we took him back to his room, frailer and lighter, and moved the bed so that he could look out of the window at the walled garden.

'I wish I had spent more time with flowers and trees and the important things of the world. I wish I could recognize those birdsongs now.'

I took it in turns with Pamela and Fitzroy to sit with him. Mrs Ross brought trays of soup and orange juice and a nurse came from Haddington to stay for the last illness. My father gave us no final instructions. He did not want to talk about his funeral or the house or the future of the estate. He sat up in bed, in a blue dressing gown Pamela had just given him, and reflected randomly on nature and Syracuse and the war in the Libyan desert. From time to time he returned to the theme of his unfinished essay.

'I think the Greeks must have got it wrong,' he said in a voice which daily became hoarser and weaker. 'Perhaps their thirst for knowledge was an unconscious desire for self-destruction.' He closed his eyes and murmured, 'Maybe it's better like this. The world needs a million years without man, a million years to recuperate.' He nodded and then opened his eyes and asked urgently, 'But do you think that's enough? How long would it take for Manhattan to topple into the sea and be buried for ever?'

He gazed out at the late summer evening. The sunlight was still strong, slanting diagonally across the lawn between the shadows of the great cedars.

'You know,' he said almost jauntily, 'I rather feel like a game of croquet.'

Then he fell asleep, the nurse came in and I went out into the garden. My father was in less pain now and seemed more at peace than I had ever seen him. Pamela came out on to the terrace and handed me a glass of whisky.

'It won't be long now,' she said.

'No.'

'Have you talked to him about the house?'

'I tried, but he changed the subject. In any case, what could he say?'

'Do you know what you're going to do?'

'Not yet.'

She breathed deeply and looked at the herbaceous border. 'Don't those tobacco plants smell marvellous! Are they *nicotiana alata*?'

'I'm afraid I don't know.'

'It's beautiful here,' she said wistfully. 'I hope you keep it.'

I went back to my father's room at nightfall. Whenever I saw him at that hour, lying calmly on the bed, lines of Eliot returned to me:

> And four wax candles in the darkened room,
> Four rings of light upon the ceiling overhead,
> An atmosphere of Juliet's tomb . . .

He woke up and the peaceful expression was transformed. It was once more the old tired face, rutted by bitterness and pain, disfigured by decades of pessimism and frustration; it reflected a life which had gone downhill ever since that Oxford double first in classics, a life wasted by humiliation and lack of achievement and also by self-pity. 'Every man's hand has been against me,' he once said in an uncharacteristic moment; but his own hands had done the most damage of all.

I was reminded of Charles V's death in the monastery at Yuste. There was the same despair that had led to withdrawal, the same agony and austerity of the final months, the renunciation of all things, not merely of ephemeral power and material possessions, but of all the values and beliefs which had guided and sustained his life.

The nurse woke me in the middle of the night, but I arrived only in time to hear my father's final intake of breath.

My aunt wiped her eyes and Fitzroy muttered, 'God rest his soul'. I was conscious only of his last breath and of the things that had gone with it, the stooped figure and the querulous voice, the pipe smoke and the classical journals, the sceptical intelligence which had been parent and partner of his unbounded pessimism. The sad tormented man who was my last Gordon ancestor had gone, leaving me an inheritance for which I had no wish.

Chapter Four

i

On an early morning in the middle of the lambing season, I parked my Landrover in the yard of Bill Lindsay's farm. It had been a terrible night, I was told, a night of high winds and horizontal rain, and the electricity cables were down in half-a-dozen places.

The young farmer was waiting in the yard with one of his collies.

'You'll be glad to be back,' he said, belting his anorak.

'Yes.' I had just arrived on the night sleeper from a week in the south. 'I'm always glad to leave London. How's it going?'

'Awful just now. At least one dead ewe and three lambs in a single night. And there's little one can do about it in this weather.' He shook his head. 'I was thinking of taking a look on the hill yonder. Would you care to come?'

'Yes, I'd love to.'

Bill Lindsay fetched a couple of crooks, handed one to me and whistled up his dog. We walked through the puddles in the steadings and then out across the meadows. Grey-faced sheep with month-old lambs scattered bleating in front of us.

'The blackface are always a problem,' he said, pointing to a flock on a higher field beyond the burn. 'Let's see how they are doing.'

We waded through the water and climbed the slope. Bill had the largest and least productive of the Starne farms, his land consisting mostly of heather and bracken with a few fields of grass near the house. As we reached the moorland, we passed a ruined cottage. I remembered my grandmother discussing its last inhabitant, a lonely old lady whom no one ever visited: she used to walk down to the village, four miles away, and post a letter to herself so that at least she could talk to the postman who delivered it the next day. The cottage had fine views of the Forth but it was a bleak unsheltered place. Close by were three hawthorns, small bent trees, defenceless against incessant gales; their contorted shape made them look as if they had been frozen in the act of attempted flight.

As the collie was herding the sheep into an angle of the top field, Bill noticed a ewe in trouble. She tried to break past the collie and he ran quickly to head her off. Skilfully catching her with his crook, he pulled her on to her back and examined her.

'She's well due,' he said, 'she'll have broken her waters some time ago.'

Holding the ewe's head firmly in one hand, he pushed his other into the sheep.

'The blessed thing's back to front,' he muttered. 'I think we'd better get it out. Can you take the head now?'

I knelt down in the moss and gripped the horns. The ewe made frightened rumbling noises, sticking out her tongue and rolling her eyes. The farmer put one hand on her stomach, trying to help with the contractions, while he pulled hard with the other. Soon the lamb's back legs appeared, yellow and slimy, and then the body slipped easily out. Bill Lindsay picked the creature up, opened its mouth and blew into it. Then he hit it and blew again.

'It's got a lot of water in its lungs,' he said.

The ewe got to her feet and sniffed at the lamb, which moved its neck slightly.

'We'll leave her,' said Lindsay, 'and hope she takes to it. But it could be tricky. It must have gulped as we took it out.'

We moved towards the rest of the flock, tramping across the marshy ground to the lowest part of the field. Bill found a sheep with foot rot and began cleaning its hoof with a penknife. I took off my coat and leant against the stone wall which separated the field from a spruce wood planted by my grandfather. Like the cottage and most of the other constructions on the estate, the wall was in need of repair. You could see it hadn't been touched for years because the brown moss was undisturbed, draped over the grey stones like the skins of great bears.

I looked back up the hill and saw that the ewe had moved away from her lamb, now an inert shape by the side of the opposite dyke.

'I think it may have died,' I said.

We ran up the slope and again the lamb tried to lift its head. Bill gave a signal to the collie and they went to fetch the ewe. But the dog moved too directly towards her and drove her further along the edge of the field. At a low point in the wall she scrambled over the loose stones and dropped on to the moor.

Bill was running again. 'Can you bring the jeep up?' he shouted.

I set off for the farmhouse and by the time I had returned Bill had the ewe by her horns. He picked her up and put her in the back of the vehicle and then went to retrieve the lamb.

'Aye, it'll be all right. The mother's an awkward one,

but if I keep them together in the shed I expect she'll take to it.'

As I drove back to Starne, I wished the other farmers and people on the estate were like Bill Lindsay. He was one of the few to whom I could talk easily, without embarrassment on either side. Perhaps it was because we were the same age and because he did not come from that region. With the others, whose families had lived there for generations, I usually felt guilty or ill-at-ease. It was awkward meeting a farmworker whom I had not seen since we had both attended the village school twenty-five years before. And I experienced uncomplicated feelings of guilt when I met the older ones, men twice my age who were driving tractors for me, men who were condemned to hours of cold and boredom in return for the minimum agricultural wage.

I tried to be friendly with all of them and called them by their Christian names. I went to their pub and talked about football and the most recent matches at Tynecastle or Easter Road. Sometimes they made a remark about politics, and I disparaged the government and made it clear I did not vote Conservative. I wanted to be an employer they liked and respected but I fear I was neither. My appearances at the pub merely caused them embarrassment and their conversations closed down when they became aware of my presence. There were similar failures of communication in the shops, where people talked to me only of the weather, and at the local garage, although there matters were made worse by my ignorance of mechanical things and my inability to recognize the most obvious types of motor car.

It was easy to develop feelings of paranoia wondering what the local people thought of me. I imagined them saying in the village, 'He's no' a patch on his grandad,' or, worse, expressing doubts about my sanity: 'The laird's no' a full shilling and that's a fact.' I realized that even my grandfather, who must have seldom spoken to working men unless it was to give them orders, would have had an easier relationship with them than I had. And doubtless they would have preferred that old-fashioned clear-cut paternalism to my ambiguous attitude of guilt mixed with good will and incomprehension.

I drove into the Starne stableyard and entered the two small rooms we called the estate office. Kirstie, the secretary, gave me a smile and the mail and said, 'Terrible weather we're having.' In the inner room the factor was seated at his desk, a large gas stove at his elbow, reading the *East Lothian Courier*.

'The prodigal son returns from the metropolis,' he announced with a wink. 'And how's yourself this wet and windy morning?'

'I've been up at Easter Cleuchhead. Bill Lindsay lost a few lambs in the night.'

'Farming's a mug's game,' he said with a grin. 'I don't know why we bother.'

Like my father, I had decided not to get rid of Logan. He was weak and incompetent but likeable, and he did not antagonize the tenants or estate workers. It was good to have someone, in that region of dour and taciturn men, who had a sense of humour, a man who interrupted even his own sentences with hearty laughter. Logan was a reassuring figure with his red face and tweed suit and permanent thirst. I knew he always had a quick dram in the office before returning to face his wife, a prim bible-clasping woman whose facial expressions alternated between anxiety and disapproval.

'And how's herself?' he asked with a chuckle. 'Is her ladyship deigning to pay a visit to these tribal parts?'

'Ellen's coming up this evening,' I said, looking through the day's post.

'Concerning matters of state,' said Logan, pronouncing each syllable slowly with mock seriousness, 'there are a number of things to report. Here is the estimate for the new barn requested by Hoggett; it seems on the steep side to me, and it's probably unnecessary. This is the report we had done for the drainage of the Cleuchhead fields. And here's a letter from the Countryside Commission with details of their revised subsidies for hardwoods.'

Kirstie came in with a tray of coffee and biscuits.

'Mrs Graham was asking again,' she said, 'if we would open the garden for her charity. I said I would talk to you.'

'We can't get the garden ready for this summer,' I answered, 'but assure her she can have it next year.'

'Isn't she delicious?' said Logan, smacking his lips after Kirstie had gone. 'I have dreams about that girl.'

She was an attractive blond woman with a friendly manner who had approached me a few weeks before and asked for a job. I wouldn't recognize her, she said with an embarrassed laugh, but we had once been friends in the village school and I used to call her 'wee girl': did I not remember how I had once protected her from spotty Jim Hoggett who now farmed at Abbey Mains? I did remember; we embraced at the recollection, and since then she had worked as our secretary while her children were at primary school.

Logan was arranging various papers.

'We have an offer from a Mr Gary Coombes,' he said peering at the signature, 'who wishes to turn Starne into a safari park. I assume the idea is redundant.'

'I don't think you need ask.'

'And then a request from a Mr Strutt to rent the grouse shooting.'

'Are there enough grouse?'

'Aye, there's the rub. To let a grouse moor in *bona fide*, one needs grouse, and there are not, I regret to say, sufficient gamebirds this year. Mr Strutt also, I note, expresses an interest in the pheasant shooting, but that's still let to friend Hoggett for the coming season.'

The previous year I had decided to ban shooting on the estate and dismiss the two keepers. To Ellen's anger I subsequently changed my mind. It was easy to take a decision like that in London, a moral decision uninfluenced by local considerations; from Starne it seemed an example of ignorant urban interference with rural ways of life. Besides, I wanted to change as little as possible. There seemed no point in having Starne if I did not preserve its links with the past and for that reason I did not wish to get rid of the surviving members of my grandparents' staff. Machale the butler was well past retirement age and none of his traditional duties remained for him to do; there wasn't even a servants' hall for him to tyrannize any longer. But he wanted to stay, frailer now and gentler, and I let him live on in his old room, still dressing up in his butler's suit and working as a part-time caretaker. The widowed Mrs Ross was another pensioner who did not want to leave, and she stayed on in the housekeeper's room, ordering the groceries and supervising the cleaning women. Starne had been her home for half a century and she would never be persuaded to retire. The finest moment of her life, she told anyone who entered the house, was the day Winston Churchill had stayed and presented her with his autograph.

'That reminds me,' Logan was saying, 'I'm afraid we are cursed with more Hoggett problems.'

I groaned excessively. 'What now?'

'Several issues outstanding, alas. One concerns the paddock where Mrs Graham keeps her grand-daughters' ponies. Apparently, this was never taken out of his father's lease, and Hoggett is now claiming compensation or its return.'

'But it's of no use to him.'

'Of course not, but you know what he's like. Perhaps it would be a good idea if you went to see him.'

I sighed. Logan could not deal with Hoggett, who openly despised him, so I would have to go myself. So much trouble had been caused over the last year by this surly farmer that I wondered whether he also remembered, and resented, my defence of Kirstie Munro in the school playground in 1954. Yet he seemed prepared to annoy anybody if his 'business', as he called his farm, required it. People often grumbled that he had ploughed up a footpath or uprooted a well-loved hedge.

Hoggett's father had been very different. He used to play the accordion and sing Harry Lauder songs in the village hall when I was a child. I remembered the way he winked as he sang,

Roamin' in the gloamin' on the banks of Clyde,
Roamin' in the gloamin' with a lassie by my side.

He had a twinkle in his eyes and loved a good dram. But his son's teetotal eyes seemed only to twinkle when he had done someone down.

'I can claim one minor achievement against Hoggett,' said Logan with a ruddy smile of satisfaction. 'Upon hearing that he aspired to election to the Conservative Club, I informed the committee that the man was no gentleman and recounted some of his misdemeanours. I am happy to say he was blackballed.'

I smiled. 'All right. I'll go and do battle at the Mains this afternoon.'

Leaving him and Kirstie, I walked over to the house. Still damp and dishevelled from the sheep incident, I went upstairs to wash and change. My wardrobe had altered over the last year. In London I had never worn a suit or a tie or a tweed jacket, but these articles were now accumulating on the old wooden coathangers in my cupboard. Some had belonged to my father, who had been much the same height, but others were new. It was somehow easier to talk to a lawyer in a tie than an open-neck shirt, easier to direct forestry operations in corduroys than blue jeans. I may have been half-conscious of my grandmother's contempt for people who walked on the moors in bright colours, for I was now usually dressed in colours of brown and green. When I looked in the mirror at my short hair and country clothes, I realized I could have passed for an actor playing a typical laird.

The children were already having lunch with Maggie, their young nanny, when I joined them in the little room we used beside the kitchen. I always had lunch or tea with them and afterwards I often took them out to one of the farms or to play hide and seek by the burn. I enjoyed those meals, sitting at the head of a table with a child on either side, listening to their childish blend of wisdom and absurdity. Other people sometimes joined us: Kirstie, if she was working in the afternoon; Logan, although he preferred to go to the pub; and Uncle Fitzroy, who came once a week. In spite of Starne's reprieve, he had opted in the end for the rest home in North Berwick. 'It's really more convenient, dear boy, for toddling on to the links.' But he came by bus every Thursday morning and wound the Starne clocks. The children adored him.

When I sat down Lucy was asking her brother to guess who was the cleverest man in the world. Stephen suggested Uncle Fitzroy because he was the oldest.

'No,' scoffed Lucy. 'God is, because he made us.'

'He didn't make me. Mummy made me. I was in her tummy.'

'But God put you there.'

They appealed to me for arbitration, the blond five-year-old girl who had my looks but seemed to have Ellen's extrovert character, and the darker three-year-old who resembled his mother but seemed like the shy introspective boy I once was.

'How did Mummy know she was having a baby?' asked Lucy. 'Did she get a letter?'

It amused me how often this type of conversation occurred. The previous Saturday we had taken our spaniel to be mated at kennels in the outskirts of Edinburgh. Lucy had asked what 'mated' meant and, when I explained it was like getting married, she enquired if we were going to take the dog to a church. I then told them what really happened and they accepted the explanation without curiosity.

I had left the dog for a few hours and taken the children into the city to look at the castle. Walking up the High Street pavement, I noticed that they avoided treading on the lines between the paving stones.

'Why are you walking like that?' I asked Lucy.

'So the bears don't get me,' she replied, and I recalled the bears and squares of the child's rhyme. Then I remembered that I too had sometimes walked in the same way without realizing why. It was one of those aspects of childhood which stay subconsciously for ever, like the technique of twisting honey on a spoon so that it does not drop on the table.

We were eating lamb cutlets for lunch.

'Who killed this sheep?' Lucy asked, picking up a bone in her fingers.

'Well, I don't know who actually killed it. We get our meat from the butcher.'

'He must have been a very nasty man.'

'No, little one, he was just doing his job.'

She looked doubtfully at me. 'Why do people have to eat sheep? Why can't they just leave them running around in the fields?'

I remembered how a week before I had told her about Easter. She had been greatly upset by the Crucifixion and had found little to console herself in the story of the Resurrection. It was Christ's death she remembered when she woke up and cried that night. 'But why did they have to kill him?' she had asked several times. 'Why did they have to put nails in him?'

Stephen finished his pudding and said suddenly, 'When's Mummy coming?'

'She'll be here before bedtime.'

Ellen and I had quarrelled, predictably, over my decision to keep Starne. But in the end we had made an arrangement which seemed to work. I lived in Scotland with the children who were now at nursery school and would soon go to the village primary; Ellen stayed in London, coming up to Starne for a couple of long weekends each month. She had rejected the plan at first, realizing only after long arguments that it suited her very well. She no longer had to look after the children or take them to play-groups and she could concentrate for most of the month on her work. Moreover, she had exacted various concessions before appearing at Starne. She would not spend any of her time there shopping or running the house; and she would not be called 'Lady Starne' by Machale or Mrs Ross or anyone else on the estate. If they would not call her Ellen, they must call her Ms Hartman.

Those had been good years for Ellen and her causes. The revolution in Lisbon had meant the end of Portuguese colonialism and her friends were now in power in Angola and Mozambique. In Angola the cause was not quite secure because the black liberation movements were fighting a civil war among themselves. But as one movement was backed by the Russians and the other by the Americans and the South Africans, it was not difficult for Ellen to know which side she was on; the posters and slogans of the MPLA still decorated the flat in Earls Court. Popular triumphs in southern Africa had been followed by more dramatic victories in south-east Asia, with much rejoicing among Ellen and her friends when the Americans and their 'lackeys' were swept from the region. Once again the victors had turned against each other and once again it was easy to decide who were the real revolutionaries and who had become genocidal deviationists backed by the West; all signs of the Khmer Rouge quickly disappeared from our London walls.

Ellen's prime interest was now Rhodesia, although she had opposed the recent talks in London on the grounds that no agreement, however satisfactory, should be made with racists. Her enthusiasm for the Third World remained undiluted and she chided me for losing mine. I admitted I had become sceptical and disillusioned, disinclined to work for the replacement of white colonialists by black tyrants who murdered the opposition and stole their country's wealth. I still worked for the same publisher, visiting him from time to time in London and bringing back a manuscript to edit or translate. But the work bored me and I planned to give it up. At the time I was translating a French book which tried to synthesize Marxism and Islam. The idea would once have interested me; it might even have been useful for certain countries. But now the thesis seemed not only dull but ridiculous. It belonged to that false London world I had thankfully given up, a world of committee meetings and badly-printed leaflets, of slogans and posters and dirty coffee mugs, of unending late-night talk about the 'struggle' and the Vietnamese 'masses'. I had problems in my life at

Starne, but they seldom provoked nostalgia for my former existence in London.

ii

I returned tired and depressed from my meeting with Hoggett. He had been more than usually obdurate, haggling over various issues, criticizing the rent review, even raising the possibility of legal action over Mrs Graham's paddock. He had also insisted on carrying out a fencing scheme of marginal value to himself which would cause considerable distress to others. On certain issues I had been forced to concede and I had noticed the mean look of satisfaction in his face. He was the worst type of eastern Scot, the sort who justified the jibes about dourness and avarice.

From my study window I looked out at the park and the great central tree which already had Dutch elm disease. A few naked branches, some leaves yellowing last August, had indicated that the giant was doomed. I wondered how long it would be before it was completely dead; three years, maybe four, and then it would have to go and its four-hundred-year mark on the landscape would go with it.

Much work still needed to be done on the estate and at that moment we still had some money to invest; the spectacular sale of the Canalettos had cleared the tax debts and left us with a small surplus. Over the previous twelve months we had made a start with the drainage and some urgent repairs of farm buildings. I had also disregarded my father's pessimism and planted new woodlands on tracts of scrubby pasture. I had spent many winter days with a group of foresters from Kelso, placing and planting thousands of young oak and beech. I had read books about trees and agriculture and I could talk about the subjects with reasonable knowledge. But I knew I was not suited for the work and my heart was not in it. I found it impossible to look at the estate as if it were a commercial asset or a business. I wanted it to stay the same, as I had always remembered it. Logan and the accountant urged me to take advantage of tax incentives the government was offering for conifer plantations on the uplands. But I could not bear to see those familiar heathered hillsides covered by alien spruce. I suppose I really wanted to have the estate without managing it, to be able to veto without having to administer. I had thought I could be happy just being there in my family home with a dog and the children and the country people, to spend my time with books and a log fire and long walks in the Lammermuir hills.

I did not want to improve that land because it had been improved too much already. Two hundred years ago the landscape had been planned by sensible and ambitious men who had drained and planted and rotated their land, making it for a time the most productive in Europe. It was bleak and efficient, with a certain beauty in its austerity and long horizontal lines, but it seemed empty of real feeling. It was a landscape without curlews, with fields too drained for snipe and hedgerows too neat for wild flowers.

Yet for me it had once been a place of mystery, a sorcerer's country, a site of remote rituals and heroic battles. And its history went back a long way before Cromwell or Queen Mary or King Edward held Dunbar. Those ancient stones on the moor were not geological curiosities but monuments of the people before the Picts, altars of sacrifice, and later the sites of Lammas bonfires and Beltane festivals. I remember old people who felt the magic and the pagan mystery, who talked of the supernatural not as an item of folklore but because they could sense it; and through them I believed as a child that I too had sensed it. But all that had gone. It was impossible to sense anything now that no one sang or told tales by the fireside.

Even in the 1950s there had been old men with laughter and stories, shepherds and keepers and ancient farmers who understood the country and the seasons and cared about the wildlife. During my years away I had thought about them involuntarily and remembered them in the poems of Stevenson and Alexander Gray. But when I returned they had died or vanished and I could not talk to their successors. The new farmers were harsh, sharp-faced men concerned only with efficiency and profit, who wanted to tear up their hedges and pull down their stone barns so that they could carve out larger fields and erect monstrous steel structures. Their wives were different too: no longer cheerful matrons in dungarees helping out with the sheep-shearing, but pretentious women like Mrs Hoggett who spent much time in the Haddington hairdresser and talked grandly of her cocktail dresses.

I went out into the garden which was always a refuge from problems. It was good to stroll there and talk to Wee Hovis about dividing the irises and other things that did not matter. He always had a cheery smile and said, whenever I had been away for more than a day, 'You'll be glad to be back.' We would talk about projects like clearing the shrubbery or replanting the orchard and then he would tell me of the minor problems which kept him awake. A pair of partridges, for example, used to nest in the park each year and bring their young into the kitchen garden to nibble at the sprouting peas. Hovis asked if we could shoot them and I refused; if necessary he could put a net over the peas. I was fond of those partridges and enjoyed finding them as I walked around the policies.

They seemed to know that the park was a sanctuary and that by staying there they were safe from the guns of Hoggett's syndicate.

iii

Ellen's train was delayed, so we were the last guests to arrive at the Haldanes'.

'Jesus!' she exclaimed as we walked through the hall, 'what a place! Where did they find all this junk?'

It was her first visit to Dundallon and she looked with amazement at the armoury of muskets and claymores arranged in geometrical patterns around the walls.

'Did they have a private army or something?'

'No, those were only in the Highlands. I imagine these weapons were collected by a Victorian ancestor.'

Dundallon had been built by a retired nabob who had spiced the opulent baronial structure with a mild oriental flavour. Cusped Moghul arches punctuated the wall of the long gallery and a magnificent howdah stood in one corner. But the dominant tone was the hunter's. Inside the arches salmon in glass cases were displayed with labels indicating their weight and date of capture. Above them were the heads of several species of antelope and the famous narwhal tusk which had masqueraded as a unicorn's horn. It was a house of alcoves and winding staircases so that one was liable to turn a corner and come face to face with the mask of an arctic fox.

'This is like a museum of Brit imperialism,' said Ellen as we passed the cane furniture and zinc-lined chests which Haldane's grandfather had brought back from India.

I had been to Dundallon several times over the previous

119

twelve months, but Ellen and Haldane had not met since Oxford twelve years before. Nevertheless, he embraced her as if they were old friends and forced her to accept a glass of champagne.

'Come along and meet some people. I don't think you know Jean and Buffy Arbuthnot, though you're practically neighbours. Hugh and Ellen Starne,' he said with a wave that included the four of us.

'Actually my name's Hartman,' Ellen told the Arbuthnots.

'I'm sorry,' said Haldane, simulating concern at a social blunder, 'I thought you were married.'

'I am, but I kept my name. Like you kept yours.'

'Yes of course,' he said genially, 'silly of me. This is Ms Hartmann,' pronouncing the title 'murz', 'crusaderess of many worthy causes and contributor to that excellent periodical we read all the time, the "New Statesperson".' He laughed as he poured more champagne. 'You'll get on frightfully well with Sir Buth here: he took rather a strong line against votes for women in about 1913. Isn't that right, Buffy?'

Arbuthnot, who was in his fifties, smiled in a way that suggested he was accustomed to his host's jibes. Haldane was as loud as he had been at Oxford but less aggressive and more affable. His career and his marriage presumably accounted for his perpetual good humour and even greater self-confidence. After a successful start as a merchant banker in London, he had charmed prim Edinburgh ladies into adopting him for my father's old constituency. 'It was dead easy,' he told me afterwards. 'I just had to memorize their names, find out a bit about their families, then talk about dogs and cats and hanging people. After that the usual spiel about the trade unions and the good old days, and Bob's your uncle. I won on the first round.' He had entered the House of Commons at the election the previous year and was now the PPS to a cabinet minister. People talked of him as if it were only a matter of time before he became secretary of state.

A tall man with a beaky nose and scarce chin came up to me with outstretched hand.

'The name's Harrington,' he said. 'We haven't met but someone just told me you've also moved up from the south. Are the natives friendly?' he asked in a feigned conspiratorial whisper.

'Well actually, I'm a sort of native myself. I was brought up here.'

'Oh dear, I am sorry. No offence I hope?'

'Of course not. Where have you moved from?'

'Hampshire. And jolly glad we were to leave. It's become Sodom and Gomorrah down there. Drugs and wife-swapping all over the place.'

'Really?'

'Yes, quite appalling. Luckily old Buffy offered me a job in his grain business. He was my commanding officer you know – hell of a long time ago now – in the Scots Guards. Only difficulty was finding a decent place to live. Did you have that problem?'

'I was fortunate to have my family's house.'

'Oh I see. Where's that?'

'It's at a place called Starne.'

'What, near that Victorian monstrosity?'

'Well, that is actually my house. But it's late Georgian mostly.'

'Oh God I'm sorry. Always putting my big feet in it. But that's a funny thing: I was told some hippie weirdo lived in it. You look pretty normal to me.'

I felt a hand between my shoulder blades steering me towards the other end of the room. Haldane said in my ear, 'Anyone who can talk to Harrington without falling asleep deserves another drink.'

'Why do you ask him then?'

'My dear fellow, in my job one has to be civil to everyone, even if they've won a medal in the Great Bores' Olympics. In any case, he's madly keen to buy our winter wheat.'

He seized a fresh bottle of champagne from the drinks tray and filled our glasses. 'Rather decent of the ancestor to lay down a dozen cases of the widow Cliquot just before he died. Now look here,' he said, changing his tone, 'have you finally agreed to let me put your name forward for the Archers?'

'You know very well I said no.'

'But for God's sake, it's the greatest fun. All one's friends come up from London and everybody gets frightfully pissed.'

In a sense it was endearing that Haldane should treat me as if we were still in the same dining club at Oxford and the intervening decade of estrangement had not occurred. But it also reflected his unnatural self-assurance and his lack of interest in other people's ideas. How could he think, knowing what I had been doing since university, that I might contemplate putting on the uniform of the royal bodyguard and strutting around Holyrood during the Queen's visits to Edinburgh?

'Well, what about the New Club then? I can put you up for that. You must have lunch somewhere when you're in Edinburgh.'

'No, I'd never use it. If I want to have lunch I go to a pub.'

'A pub?'

'Yes, why not? Anyway, I shouldn't think the New Club would elect me after the way it was treated by my family.'

The resignations of both my father and my grandfather had been publicized in the press: my father's in a letter to the *Scotsman* criticizing the demolition of the old premises, my grandfather's originally in a gossip column and then repeated in many places as an example of his eccentricity. He was resigning, he solemnly told the committee, because the brussels sprouts were overcooked.

My cousin Clarissa came up and embraced me. 'Aren't you going to introduce me to your wife? Isn't it about time after all these years?'

Clarissa had always been beautiful; even as a teenager she had managed to avoid acne and puppy fat. She had evolved from the thin ethereal child to the mature woman without anyone being able to say, 'What a pity she's going through this stage. She was such a pretty little thing.' She used to disparage her adult form, saying it resembled too closely the shape of her cello, but she was widely regarded as the most attractive woman in the district. Someone once compared her to a Scott Fitzgerald character, immaculate and unapproachable, capable of concealing every emotion except boredom. Perhaps he had a point: those relentless green eyes in their white marble face could, intentionally or otherwise, freeze people. But I had known them all my life and was immune to that danger. It seldom took more than the opening sentences before we were back in our childhood, when I thought she would be the only woman in my life.

'I hope I'm going to like her because I could still sue you for breach of promise. I can remember at least five occasions between the age of nine and fourteen when you proposed marriage; and each time I accepted. But then you started falling for anything in a skirt and you abandoned me.'

'That isn't true. I was faithful for much longer than you. I used to get jealous at teenage dances and sulk if you went off with other boys. I remember trying to ridicule them afterwards.'

'To you I was just one of the harem.'

'Do you remember the Cuban missile crisis? I was fourteen then and I believed in a rather esoteric form of reincarnation, convinced that everyone who died came back in the next life as the exact opposite. I remember the night I asked my housemaster if we were all going to die in a nuclear war, and he said that of course we mustn't panic but things did look pretty ominous. And afterwards I prayed and prayed that there would be no war because if you had died you would have come back as ugly, fat and stupid – and male of course – and you would be living in a mud hut in Africa. I swear that was my only concern.'

She laughed. 'That's such a mad story that I suppose I must believe it. But you still abandoned me.'

'Fortunately for you. Because instead of marrying a crazy cousin with hang-ups and an identity crisis, you married the Coming Man of the 1980s. By the turn of the century you'll be queening it over Downing Street.'

She had married Haldane five years before and already they had three sons. It was one of the few marriages in the district which everyone agreed was a success, and all tried to catch them for their dinner parties.

'I remember that you didn't come to our wedding,' she said. 'I hoped at the time it was because it would be too painful for you. But I didn't believe that was the real reason.'

'I'm afraid it wasn't. We were in Lourenço Marques then, visiting Samora Machel and the Frelimo government.'

There were eighteen at dinner, the Haldanes presiding at either end of the long mahogany table. I sat down smiling, remembering my grandmother's injunctions about dinner parties: 'It doesn't matter how many guests,' she used to say, 'so long as it's even numbers and you can't divide by four. Otherwise you don't have the host and hostess sitting at the ends.'

Mrs Arbuthnot said to me, 'I hear you play the piano.'

'Well, not really. Only to myself.'

'Come now, don't be coy. I know you won the piano competition at Eton.'

'Only the junior cup, and everyone said it was a fluke. But how did you know?'

'A little bird told me,' she said, winking towards Clarissa. 'Now do tell me what you like to play. Whose spirit do you feel you interpret best?'

'I really don't know. I like, for example, some things of Debussy, most of Chopin, and then there's . . .'

She raised a hand to dismiss Debussy. 'He has no messages for me because he was not *inspired*. But as for Chopin, oh Chopin! I always think of him as the nightingale of composers, don't you?'

'I doubt I could recognize a nightingale. How do they sing?'

'To tell you the truth, I'm not sure either. But it must be delightful, don't you think? I mean, Keats couldn't have got it wrong, could he? I think one can trust Keats.'

The woman on my other side was no more promising and before long we were talking about her horses, her children and her knitwear business. I couldn't recall her name but I remembered the previous occasion we had met, thirteen years before, at a dinner before a coming-out dance. And I remembered her exact words: 'I don't see the point of going to university. Surely, if one has an estate, it's better to go into the army and learn to give orders.' It had been said in Britain in 1967, during Harold Wilson's second Labour government, in the same blasé uncomprehending tone in which she now discussed gymkhanas.

From the end of the table I could hear that Ellen and

Haldane had returned to the topic of maiden names.

'But why should women be deprived of their identity just because they marry?'

I knew how Ellen's argument would develop. There would be references to Iceland and Norway, where apparently the women keep their father's name, and to Spain, where children are given both their parents' surnames. But the mother's family still disappeared, even if it was with her grandchildren rather than her children. In London I had conformed to the dictates of feminist jargon so that in committee meetings I was even able to refer to the 'chairperson' without laughing. But it now seemed absurd and unimportant, and the intransigence of Ellen and her friends merely alienated people who would otherwise have supported the campaign for equal rights.

I was nervous of the after-dinner port ritual because this would give Ellen a further opportunity to make a fuss and have an argument. But in the end she made only a minor demonstration, arguing about Iceland for a mere three minutes after Clarissa had stood up.

While Haldane circulated the port – 'most thoughtfully laid down by the ancestor' – Harrington and Arbuthnot moved into the chairs on either side of me. They lit up cigars, apologized for talking across me and reminisced about their years in the Scots Guards and more recent occasions shooting pheasants. Occasionally they tried to bring me into the conversation, on these and other subjects of which I had no experience. But I was happy to sit back and not take part. It was incredible, really, how conformist this society was, all these men with similar backgrounds and similar careers and the same interests and the same politics. There were no political deviants among them. Not only were they all Conservatives; they all believed that until then Conservative governments had been too left-wing. Listening to their views and accents, you might think you were in the Home Counties. They were not interested in Scotland and knew nothing about it except a few fables of its history, a few lines of Burns and a couple of salmon rivers. None of them apart from Haldane would have heard of James Maxton or John Mclean, and they would have all dismissed Mick McGahey as a foreign agent. For them Scotland's other classes were ghillies and grocers whom they regarded as cardboard Harry Lauder figures, stock characters in an unchanging world of shooting and stalking and other pastimes of the squire.

On the drive home Ellen declared that she would never go to another dinner party in Scotland.

'Those guys are just morons. Haldane's different: he may be a fascist but he's quite bright. The others are a bunch of doughheads.'

'Look, you know basically I agree with you. But surely you didn't have to be so abusive at the end?'

There had been an embarrassing row about abortion in which she had splattered Harrington with obscenities and called him a lunkheaded dumbbell.

'That jerk just made me want to throw up. Did you hear him telling me that a woman's place was in the home and our duty was to have kids? In 1980 for Christ's sake!'

It was one o'clock when we reached Starne but I was not tired and I went alone into the drawing room. On a sudden whim I lit the candles on the mantelpiece and carried them over to the piano. I found the book of nocturnes and sat down to play the slow rhapsodic opening of the first G-minor. But I stumbled over the chords of the *religioso* section and stopped and closed the lid. I had remembered the stupid woman who said Chopin was a nightingale.

I rose, opened a shutter and stared out into the blackness. I wished I could understand this mood of elemental discontent, this disquiet which loomed and faded and yet was always there. I felt guilty as well as perplexed that it afflicted me and not people with serious problems. An old woman who worked in the laundry in Haddington had a husband with multiple sclerosis. She had been living with the disease for a dozen years, witnessing the long deterioration, but she was always serene and cheerful; she never became angry even with difficult and complaining customers. And I, who had most of what I wanted, could find serenity nowhere.

I walked aimlessly around the room which had once smelt of immense lilies. They had stood in the *cache-pots* and *jardinières* which in winter had been occupied by hyacinths and chrysanthemums and ranks of white cyclamen. I remembered particularly the blue hyacinths and the dense cloying smell when they were over. There were no flowers and no smells now; some pot-pourri remained in *sang-de-boeuf* bowls but it was scentless and crumbling. The red silk brocade on the walls had become tattered in places but the heavy damask curtains were still in fine condition. A quarter of a century before, my grandmother had found the new material too bright and they had been laid out in the summer sun to fade. I remembered their being hung up afterwards and the rustling noise they made as they billowed gently across the floor.

The drawing room was like a memorial, beautiful and purposeless, a space which was never used and hardly ever seen, where the ormolu clock never ticked and the satin chairs were never creased. Its centre was dominated by a great fireplace where the logs were never lit, and at either end stood heavy *boule* desks at which nobody ever sat to write a letter or a journal. Even the faded red curtains had no function; at night the shutters were closed and during summer the blinds came down to preserve the room from the sun. But what was it being preserved for? These relics which had no use for me could not conceivably be useful to my successors.

I wandered back to the piano and picked up the book of songs my mother used to play from after tea. I leafed through it, looking at the pictures of John Peel and the Minstrel Boy and the British Grenadiers. Each song conjured up a different memory of childhood, and I recalled which were my favourites and which were my mother's. I had hated 'The Campbells are coming', even though it was a beautiful song, because the Campbells were on the English side and had stolen the lands of the Jacobite chiefs.

I closed the book with a sigh and put it away. Again I remembered Mrs Arbuthnot and her gushing remark about Keats and the nightingale. Scattered lines skimmed across my memory, fragments of the ode seeming suddenly to explain the feelings of futility and discontent.

> Thou wast not born for death, immortal Bird!
> No hungry generations tread thee down;

And yet they trod me unceasingly. I realized I was no longer leading a life of the present but a series of expeditions into the past, a constant search for lost memories which were better left interred. My old books and toys acquired magical properties in remembrance, but on discovery they were transformed into banal objects. I thought I had loved the great wooden chest in the kitchen, remembering with nostalgia the labels on its drawers indicating nutmeg and tapioca and Indian arrowroot. But when I saw it again after many years, it was just a chest, the sort of object one looks at with mild curiosity in an antique shop.

It was absurd, I thought, to have spent my childhood

longing to be a grown-up living in another part of the world and then to live as an adult trying to recreate the past. In any case, it was difficult to live a real life in that house where I was more of a tenant or a temporary lodger than the owner. At Starne I seemed to be not an individual but one of a line of curators whose sole function was to conserve, preserve and hand over the property in as good a condition as possible. And yet my ancestors had not had to live like me. They had enjoyed their lives and consumed without being forced to worry about the family heritage. My tenancy of Starne was different: it was a castrated existence. I was not the sultan of the palace, nor even the grand vizier, but the chief eunuch preserving its harem-less walls against the modern world.

Chapter Five

i

During that year and the one after I went often to Dundallon. On Sundays when Ellen was in the south, I drove the children over for lunch and on summer evenings I sometimes walked there alone. It took little more than an hour by the footpath which left the Starne woods and ran through banks of yellow broom before cutting across a stretch of moorland and ending in the brackened slopes above the Haldanes' house.

I grew to like that house with its extravagant collections of weapons and trophies, the moose heads on the stairs and the fish in their glass cases. There was always a good welcome, a log fire even in summer, and the smells of cooking and juniper wood. And there were two people whom I had once been very close to who did much to mitigate the solitude of my life at Starne.

Haldane was now a junior minister, the youngest in the government, but on Sundays he saw little need to work on the coming week's agenda. His constituency duties were over by midday on Saturday and for the next thirty-six hours he could relax with his family. When I arrived in the evenings, I usually found him playing soldiers with his eldest son; on the floor by his plywood castle he guarded a plate of oatcakes and a glass of malt whisky.

We greeted each other as old friends, both of us recognizing, I think, that we were really friends of the past rather than of the present. We called each other by our surnames, as we had done since our schooldays; indeed, he still called me Gordon although my name had changed with my grandfather's death and again with my father's. We laughed together and drank whisky and got on well, but we both realized the friendship was grounded in the past. We had little in common now, and it was difficult to find subjects we could agree on. It was easier to recall episodes of university life, the time he threw a beer mug at a Trinity window, the night we climbed the clock tower and hung the Union Jack on the minute hand.

'Do you remember,' he said one night, 'that splendid evening at the Grid when I gave Middleton odds of nine to four that he couldn't run naked to Carfax and back without being caught by the police?'

'And did he make it?' Clarissa asked indulgently.

'No, the rozzer nabbed him inches from the winning post.'

But with Clarissa it was different. The past was of course important and we too talked of the experiences we had shared in childhood and adolescence. Yet with us it formed merely the background of a new friendship based on present interests and feelings. As her husband spent much of his week in Westminster, we often saw each other alone. Wednesday was her day in Edinburgh and we used to meet for lunch in a restaurant in Hanover Street and visit a gallery afterwards. We went for evening walks in the Lammermuirs and sometimes I stayed at Dundallon for supper. After the meal she brought out her cello and we sat late into the night practising the

Brahms cello sonatas. Clarissa particularly loved the later work which she said was the more romantic. I preferred the earlier, more lyrical E minor, whose opening bars I came to think of as a sort of theme tune for our friendship. I loved to watch her stirring her bow through those deep early phrases while I accompanied her with light chords on the piano.

As neither of us had many friends in the district, we depended a good deal on each other. It was natural, therefore, that she should telephone me the Saturday her crisis broke.

'Please come over,' she said in a voice taut with desperation. 'Something terrible's happened and I can't cope by myself.'

'But what is it? Tell me.'

'I can't explain on the telephone. Nobody's dying or anything like that. But it's quite ghastly.'

'Isn't Roddy there?'

'Yes, but it's even worse for him. Can't you come now?'

'I'll come immediately.'

As I parked on the Dundallon gravel, Aunt Pamela came down the steps with her three grandchildren. Stern eyes and a down-turned mouth indicated censorious disapproval.

'What's happened?' I asked her.

Grasping the two younger boys by the hand, she shook her head.

'You'd better ask Clarissa. She's in the sitting room.'

The nanny followed them out with a suitcase and a bag of teddy bears which she put in the boot of a car.

'Tell her,' commanded my aunt from the driving seat, 'to ring me this evening. But I think it's better that I should keep the boys for a while.'

Clarissa was sitting on a sofa with her face in her hands.

She looked up when I entered, her streaked face indicating recent tears.

'My God, what's the matter?'

She embraced me and began to sob.

'It's all so awful. I don't know what we're going to do.'

The telephone rang and she went over to answer it.

'I'm afraid Sir Roderick is not in,' she said into the mouthpiece. 'No, it's not. Lady Haldane has also gone out. I don't know when they will be back. Goodbye.'

She clenched her fists and looked up to the ceiling.

'The monstrous press are ruining Roddy's career and our lives and everything. Do you mind answering the telephone and telling those scavengers we're not here?'

'Of course not. But why don't you leave it off the hook?'

'Because it may be important. The Scottish Office may ring. Or the chairman of the party. Or even, oh God, even Downing Street.'

'It's that serious?'

'I'm afraid it is. Roddy's saying he'll have to resign. He's gone and got himself involved in some scandal that's about to break. A sex scandal which will be all over the Sunday newspapers.'

She collapsed on the sofa and asked me to get her a drink.

'I know it's early but I must have something to stop me shaking. Anything, vodka if it's there, but please make it strong.'

I poured out a drink and sat down beside her. It was the first time I had seen her uncomposed. Her pale face was flushed in places, her hair dishevelled and a muscle twitched in one cheek. She held the glass in one nervous hand and in the other clutched a handkerchief.

'Some horrid tart has gone to the press with photographs and one of those disgusting rags has bought her story. Imagine what it will be like tomorrow morning. Huge photographs of her and Roddy and horrible details of where they met and what they did. It'll be dreadful and humiliating and the end of everything. We'll never be able to look anyone in the face again.'

'Of course it will be embarrassing for a time. But Parliament breaks up at the end of next month and by the autumn people will have forgotten about it.'

She shook her head and gulped her drink.

'He thinks he'll have to resign this week.'

'But why? He's not in the ministry of defence. He hasn't lied to the House of Commons. I don't imagine he's being blackmailed by the Russians.'

'No, none of that.'

'Well then, he can ride it out. It's not a crime. It's a matter for embarrassment but not for resignation.'

'I don't know.' She sighed long, and then sniffed and closed her eyes. 'Well yes I do actually. God, if it's difficult to tell you, what's it going to be like when the whole world knows?' She now blushed and put her hand over her eyes. 'Apparently this tart told the journalists that Roddy has unusual tastes and didn't like to sleep with her normally. So they're going to brand him a pervert as well – which he isn't, at least not with me.'

Her fears were realized next day by headlines in the popular press. One article entitled 'Soddy Roddy' included an interview with the prostitute and a photograph of her sticking out that part of her anatomy which had allegedly attracted Haldane.

I drove over to Dundallon after breakfast and found the Haldanes with a libel lawyer in the library.

'Thank goodness you've come,' said Clarissa. 'Do you mind resuming your post by the telephone?'

I went into the sitting room and spent the morning answering the calls of journalists, friends and a couple of

lunatics. Haldane came in twice to pour himself tumblers
of neat whisky.

'Any luck with the lawyer?' I asked.

'Bloody hopeless,' he muttered. 'There are a few minor
inaccuracies but nothing worth a writ. That bitch was
using a tape recorder as well as getting her pimp to take
photographs.'

By lunchtime he was drunk and truculent and dismis-
sive of all advice.

'There's no need to resign your seat,' I told him, 'even
if you have to leave the government. The constituency
party can't get rid of you and there won't be an election
for two or three years. By then they'll have forgotten it.'

'Nonsense,' replied Haldane. 'You know nothing
about middle-class middle-aged Edinburgh ladies. They
are obsessed by sexual respectability. They would faint
at the thought of their own conception.'

While serving himself at the sideboard, he dropped his
plate and it broke. Swearing loudly, he kicked the bits
aside but made no attempt to pick them up.

'What the hell's wrong with a bit of experimenting?' he
asked, sitting down with a fresh plate and helping himself
to more whisky. 'Most couples try it, according to the
statistics. Though you would never let me,' he added
aggressively to Clarissa. 'And fifteen per cent, that's about
one in six, do it regularly. I've read that.' He turned and
wagged a finger in my direction. 'That means a hundred
people in the House of Commons are doing it – more if
you count the bloody queers. A hundred sodomizing
MPs, and I'm the only one who gets punished for it.'

'Well, be defiant then. Stand up to the Edinburgh
ladies.'

'It's all very well for you to talk like that. You've
decided never to do anything worthwhile with your life.
But I couldn't carry on a career after this; it would always

be counted against me. Somerset Maugham once said that everyone's sex life contained things which, if broadcast, would disgust everyone else. And he was right, if you exclude frigid Edinburgh ladies who don't have sex lives. But the point is that everyone doesn't know how kinky everyone else is, and therefore careers don't get buggered up except by bloody bad luck.'

The following day he resigned from the government and released a short statement to the press. It contained nothing about his future as an MP, though there had been some speculation in the morning papers and his constituents were reported 'to take a dim view'. A couple declared in a radio interview that they did not want to be represented by a pervert.

I drove over in the afternoon, past the crowd of photographers at the Dundallon gates, and returned each day that week. I saw little of Haldane, who spent most of the time drinking whisky in his study. If Clarissa or I tried to comfort him, he usually snarled and told us to go to hell. So we sat together in the sitting room, playing backgammon and answering the telephone. Other friends dropped in, but Haldane refused to see them.

'What's he been like today?' I asked on the fifth day of the crisis.

Clarissa's dice scuttled over the cork board and she moved two white pieces towards her corner.

'Awful,' she answered, sweeping her hair back in a characteristic tired gesture. 'And I don't just mean drunk and aggressive and slamming doors. But vicious and irrational as well. He hates me now. Perhaps he hates you too, even though we're the two people who are doing most to help him.'

'But how can he hate you?'

'I don't know. He just does. This afternoon he even blamed me for what happened.'

'How could he?'

She smiled slightly, reluctant to explain. 'Because he's not in his right mind. He said that if I had let him do it that way to me, then he wouldn't have needed to do it with that frightful whore. It's my fault, apparently, that it became a fixation for him. But that only shows you how completely irrational he is now.'

'Can't you take him away?'

'Where to?'

'Somewhere abroad. Somewhere where people won't recognize him. Somewhere where he has something to do other than brood. I don't know. What about a safari?'

'Maybe.' She shrugged her shoulders. 'But he'll have to stay until the constituency decides what it's going to do. Not that he's got a chance,' she added. 'The venom in these people is unbelievable.'

ii

The following week Haldane resigned from the House of Commons and two days later he took his family to a rented villa near Genoa. They planned to stay for a month but after a week Clarissa returned to Scotland with the children.

'It was a disaster,' she said the next day at our usual restaurant in Edinburgh. 'I should have come home within forty-eight hours but I kept thinking the sun and the wine might change him for the better. They didn't, they made him worse. I didn't realize people get drunk in different ways, depending on what they drink. With whisky he was usually sullen and disagreeable, but with wine he became violent. As you can see,' she added with a forlorn smile, indicating the magenta bruise under her left eye.

'And it wasn't just with me. He quarrelled with every-body. He was always insulting people in restaurants, particularly if they were Germans. Once, when he dis-covered there was a party of Dutch in the same place, he went up to their table and made a little speech. Can you imagine what he said? He told them the Dutch were so hideous he didn't understand how they managed to reproduce. It was so embarrassing – you know how the Dutch speak perfect English – that I just fled. Another time he punched a waiter in Portofino and it was even worse. Tables and chairs went over, plates were smashed; it was like one of the saloon bar scenes in a Western. He was lucky not to be arrested. Even so, I had to pay half a million lire to the manager before we could get away in a taxi.'

'So you decided to come home.'

'Well, it was his decision too. He said he wasn't going to spend the rest of the summer being harassed by "huns" and he had decided to move somewhere else – alone. I've no idea where he is now. At different times he talked of going to South Africa or the Caribbean. He said he would cable his lawyers when he got to his destination and I could find out from them where he was.'

'Of course, it's a terrible tragedy for him. But I don't understand why he's so nasty to you.'

'Not just to me.' She shook her head slowly and fiddled with a toothpick. 'To everybody, to the world. He's gone completely to pieces. You see, nothing had ever gone wrong before. There were no setbacks, no defeats. Do you remember what he was like when we were children? He wasn't shy like we were, he was the best shot among the boys, he danced reels better than any of us. And it was like that all the way along, at Eton and Oxford and until last month at Westminster. He was always successful – in sport, with women, with whatever work interested

139

him. And now his entire world has been smashed and he can't take it.

'For most people life is like snakes and ladders. You have your advances and your setbacks, but most of the time you're inching forward. But Roddy just charged up all the ladders and when he got to the top he was swallowed by the biggest snake of all – a snake so long it doesn't appear on most people's boards. He's now right at the bottom and he'll stay there. Of course he might climb the little ladders, he could become a businessman, he could get a good job in a bank. But he won't do it because it was once beneath him. He will go through life brooding on his tragedy and one day he may kill himself or, more likely, drink himself to death. If he comes back, I'll look after him and encourage him to do something. But it won't work. He's like a man with a death wish.'

After lunch we walked up Salisbury Crags and sat on a rock overlooking Holyrood Palace and the old grey city. Seagulls floated around us and runners in shorts toiled up the footpath behind. From the brewery at the bottom of the Royal Mile came a pungent smell of malt.

'Is this where that German threw his wife off for the insurance policy?' asked Clarissa.

'I don't know. It looks a bit risky to me. One might bounce down those rocks and still survive.'

She stretched herself face down on the grass, her chin propped on her hands.

'Thank goodness people know we are cousins. Otherwise we wouldn't be able to have lunch without their assuming we were having an affair. I hate the fact that one can't become friends of other men up here; one has to do everything in couples. If you're seen with another man – even if you meet him by accident out shopping – people start gossiping. Edinburgh's a goldfish bowl society.'

I gazed down at that strange beautiful city, the miles of classical buildings smudged grey with coal smoke, the miles of doomed elms, the miles and miles of iron railings guarding rigid traditions of respectability. I saw the distant buses, maroon-white or green, moving slowly along Princes Street, and I thought of the secretaries who would soon emerge from their offices, crowding on to the pavements and swelling the bus queues in Charlotte Square. And then I thought of Roddy Haldane's constituents, the seventy thousand adults down there in the city, seventy thousand people who would remember him for one thing above all others.

'Were you as happy as everyone thought?' I asked.

'Not really. I know they always said we had everything, including the perfect marriage. But it wasn't true. I think we were reasonably happy – he certainly was – but I had lost all illusions long before this happened. I found out ages ago that he was unfaithful – and with a friend of mine, not just a tart. I minded at first and thought of beginning a revenge affair; but there was nobody I wanted to have an affair with. And anyway I soon realized that infidelity wasn't the most important thing. I know he enjoyed having a mistress; it helped massage his ego, but he was far too self-absorbed to want to divorce me so that he could marry her. The fact was that all women were unimportant to him and therefore I, the mother of his children, was safe. So the problem was his selfishness and his thoughtlessness. I didn't particularly mind his forgetting my birthday or our wedding anniversary. It was just his attitude, his disregard for my feelings that hurt, his assumption that my views didn't matter. And in that way he was like most of the other men who live in the mansion houses and former manses of the Lothians, men who don't really like being with women. Most of that class prefer to be with a gun or a billiard cue or a glass of port. Women with minds scare them. They can't talk to us, can't even look us properly in the eyes.'

'But Roddy isn't like that.'

'He's really happier in his club, you know. He doesn't care for what he calls brainy girls.'

'Yes, I remember now. He once told me he preferred debs.'

'It's your wretched education,' she said with a smile.

We stayed there on the summit until a cool breeze came up from the Forth. Clarissa shivered and said she should go back to Dundallon to see the children.

'Have you made any plans?' I asked, as we walked down the footpath.

'Just to carry on. Take the children to the beach. Read them a story. Tuck them up at night. What else can I do? I can't afford a nervous breakdown.'

Her resilience surprised me. Perhaps they were partly right, those people who complained she was hard and unemotional. I could picture her at the Haldane home, carrying on as if nothing had happened: no ranting, no hysteria, no tearful confidences to sympathetic friends. Yet I wondered whether this poise was contrived, a mask against the world, a barricade set up to repel demonstrations of pity and intimacy.

'If you don't want to spend the whole of August at Dundallon, you could come with us to the west coast. I have rented a little cottage on an island off Skye for a fortnight. It might be quite fun. I don't know much about the place except that it's very small and primitive. No telephone, no electricity, a typical two-up two-down crofter's cottage. But we could take camp beds and fit in all the children.'

'You managed to persuade Ellen to go to a place like that?'

'Well, she was reluctant. She wanted to go abroad but I said the children were too young to swelter in the Mediterranean. So she agreed to go to Raasay, although she knows she'll hate it. She won't be able to buy a newspaper or watch the news on television. She won't know what's going on in Nicaragua or Afghanistan or the Iran–Iraq war. It'll be a disaster,' I laughed, 'so why don't you come instead and give her a reprieve? She won't feel guilty about not going if she knows the children have their cousins to play with.'

iii

Clarissa loved Raasay. She loved the croft at the end of the rough track, with its burn of brown peaty water and the small reeded loch where we disturbed a black-throated diver. She loved the little house with its oil lamps, its gas cylinders and the stack of peat that was its only form of heating. And she loved the enthusiasm of the five children, their excitement on the ferries and their delight in discovering the geography of this remote crofting outpost.

'What a wonderful place,' she exclaimed as we walked after supper on the hillside behind the house. 'It really is lucky people know we are cousins,' she laughed. 'Otherwise they would think it was a love nest.'

'Not if they knew we were in a two-bedroomed croft with five children and a nanny.'

From the summit the view stretched across the Sound of Raasay to the dark silhouette of eastern Skye. There were the grouped peaks of the Cuillins to the south, with Staffin Bay and the Trotternish cliffs to the west. Farther out, and paler towards the sunset, we could see the indistinct shapes of the Outer Hebrides.

'I'm so happy here,' she said, taking my arm. 'I knew I would be, as soon as I heard the boatmen speaking Gaelic. It's so wonderful not having telephones or television. I feel I have escaped, for the first time since the ordeal began, and nobody can touch me here.'

'Not even your husband?'

She shrugged. 'I told his lawyer where I am, so he can come here if he wants. But I don't think he will,' she said, gripping my arm harder, 'and I don't want him to.'

Next morning we left the children with Maggie and took the ferry back to Skye to buy provisions. We drove to Portree and bought food from half a dozen small shops. Clarissa enjoyed the release from supermarkets and the leisure to ask fishmongers about the varieties of fish and the ways of cooking them. Sometimes, even after we had bought things, she stayed in a shop just to listen to the Gaelic of other customers.

'If Roddy doesn't come back,' she announced on the way home with a half-serious laugh, 'I'll learn Gaelic and take up painting and settle here. Do you think it's a good idea?'

We collected the children and took them for a picnic on the beach beside the lighthouse on the south-east corner of the island. Afterwards they paddled and dug castles in the sand and we gazed at the hills of Applecross and watched oyster-catchers swooping over the shore line. Later I built a high peat fire at the croft and we sat crosslegged in front of it drinking Skye whisky.

'We are just cousins, aren't we?' she asked with a faint smile when Maggie and the children had gone to bed.

'Yes, just good cousins,' I laughed and kissed her on the cheek.

But an hour later we were lovers. Perhaps there had always been some self-deception in the cousinly relationship; even as children we had been more than cousins.

We were always touching each other, as relations often do, but not with the same feelings. And yet it had been neither planned nor expected. If in the past the idea had occurred to me, I had rejected it as neither possible nor desirable. I had sometimes thought wistfully that I would have married her if she had not been my cousin. But the blood tie, the half-sisterly attachment, convinced me we would never be lovers.

And yet it happened, unasked and unpremeditated, on the shabby rug in front of the peat fire. We had been sitting on the floor, murmuring the lines of a Scots ballad, when Clarissa suddenly smiled and stretched out her legs. And I bent forward and took her in my arms, and we made love gently and silently on that threadbare rug. Afterwards, as I lay holding her, my eyes in her hair, I felt, absurdly, that she had been mine since childhood, eternally mine from the past and into the future, and her marriage had been only an interlude in our love. We said nothing because nothing except banalities could be said. I looked into her tearful smiling eyes and smiled back at them and she shook her head as if in disbelief. We made love once more and then she stood up without a word and went upstairs to her children.

Neither of us mentioned it the next morning, so that the whole thing seemed like a dream, conjured from the enchanted fumes of peat and the heady malt whisky of Talisker. Yet her laughter and her eyes without remorse showed that our love-making was not the product of a sudden bewitchment, a solitary moment summoned by a sorcerer's spell. We took the children again to the sea and after a picnic lunch we left them to gather shells on the foreshore. The hillside behind was freckled by crouched rowans and we climbed between them until we reached a marshy plateau. We took our shoes off to walk across the sphagnum moss and then we sat down by a small burn which twisted down to the sea. The sun had dried the grass banks and the place smelt faintly of bog myrtle and sheep's wool.

'A book of verses underneath the bough,' whispered Clarissa, 'a jug of wine, a loaf of bread, and thou beside me, singing in the wilderness. . . .'

'But no wine nor bread nor even verses,' I answered, 'just thou and the wilderness.'

'It's enough.'

We stretched out on the grass and this time she did not attempt to suppress the sounds and movements of her love-making. We lay together for a long time and I thought there would never be another moment quite like this. It seemed almost too perfect. There were no flies, no midges, no sounds but the skylarks and the gurgling burn and the rustle of the warm breeze which lightly touched our bodies.

'I woke up this morning,' she said afterwards, 'and thought, My God! I'm an adulteress, a fallen woman. At the age of thirty-two and after only six years of marriage, I have become another man's mistress.' But she said it without regret and that night we abandoned the fireside and took two rugs up the slope behind the croft and lay under the stars until the dawn gathered beyond the mainland.

The idyll lasted three or four days before it was marred by her remorse. At first this was not serious, consisting of scattered reflections of doubt and partial guilt. But later it became insistent and almost obsessive as she racked herself with excuses and accusation.

'Should I be true to myself or true to the upbringing I had and the vows I once made? Which is the greater infidelity?'

We lay one afternoon beside the burn, staring without focus at a cloudless sky.

'Sometimes,' she mused, 'I think I'm a romantic lady with a lover and sometimes I think I'm just a whore.'

'Don't be silly. You are a romantic lady. No whore would behave like this.'

'Perhaps I am worse than a whore. Abandoning my husband when he's down. Is there anything worse than that, anything more disloyal?'

'He abandoned you first.'

I closed my eyes. I was sleepy after the wine we had drunk at lunch and didn't want to continue the conversation. Clarissa sat up and began to entwine grass stems.

'Words like "mistress" and "adultery" keep coming into my head, words that before I had only associated with other people. And now I realize they mean me. I am unfaithful, I am an adulteress, I have broken the seventh commandment.'

'There's no need to be dramatic about it. I expect you've broken the third and fourth as well. So have the rest of us.'

'It's all very well for you to be flippant. You've done it before. I haven't, so it's different. I feel guilty and frightened and sometimes I hate myself.'

I sat up too and watched the water trickling down the hillside. I remembered that as a child I used to wonder whether the world was so organic that its history could be deduced from a drop of water. Could an intelligence a billion times greater than Einstein's read its history through that minute evidence? I remembered too how I used to stare at flowing water and then look quickly at the bank so that for a moment it seemed that the land was moving in the opposite direction. That was like being in a train at a railway station; as the coaches on the other platform moved off, you thought it was your train that was leaving.

Clarissa disturbed me with harsher words.

147

'Don't think I have any illusions about you. I once saw you with a woman coming out of that motel off the Dalkeith Road and I thought how sordid you had become. No longer the romantic who used to write music for me, but someone who gives false names in cheap hotels so that he can spend a couple of hours with some pathetic woman – a woman who then has to rush back to collect her children from school and pretend to her husband that everything is normal.'

I made no attempt at justification because I hoped she would drop the subject. She did, but later at the cottage, when the children had gone to bed and Maggie had driven to the island's youth hostel, she brought it up again.

'I hate your indiscriminate availability. It's so cheap. And it makes me feel cheap too.'

'I am not indiscriminate, I am not available, and I love you very much. You're the only person in the world I want to be with.'

'At the moment,' she snorted. 'Until someone else comes along.'

'That's not true.'

'It's why Roddy resents you so much now. He said you were a worse womanizer than he is, but he's the one who suffered for it.'

'I never went with prostitutes.'

'There are worse crimes than that,' she said bitterly. 'After he had broken up with his mistress, he didn't want to become involved in another affair. It was something physical he needed, reprehensible perhaps, but it didn't damage other people. He left no casualties, he didn't play with the emotions of vulnerable women.'

'Neither do I.'

She gestured disdainfully with her hand and listed five names.

'I did not have affairs with all of them. And with the

others it was a mutual decision. We all knew what the limits were.'

'That makes no difference. They didn't know how they would be hurt. You did, because you had seen it happen before.'

I remained silent, conscious that she was partly right. Some women with disintegrating marriages undoubtedly had viewed me as a possible solution. They had seen me in that great house, nearly alone, with a strange and surely unsatisfactory marriage, and perhaps they had thought they would find salvation as mistress of Starne. Maybe they had confused love with aspiration, and their pain owed more to failed ambition than to unreciprocated feelings. But certainly, as Clarissa implied, there had been some casualties.

I said, 'If you don't want to go up the hill when Maggie gets back, let's go to sleep now. There's no point discussing things that happened a long time in the past. You knew about them when we first made love ten days ago and nothing has changed since then.'

She brushed the crumbs of peat towards the fire, sweeping them carefully under the grate so that no trace remained on the hearth.

'I'm sorry,' she said, slowly replacing the brush in its corner. 'I know nothing's changed. But the day after tomorrow we are going home and then everything will change. It will be back to real life and I don't know if that life includes my husband or not. I don't even know if I want him to come back. I came here with awful problems which you have helped me to forget for a few days. But I know very well that I am returning with those problems intact – and an extra one as well.'

She moved beside me on the rug and kissed me. 'Of course I want to go up the hill. I don't want to miss a single minute with you, even if it means retribution and God knows what at the end. I'm sorry if I criticize you, but perhaps I do it because I'm afraid of loving you too much.'

She put her arms around my knees and rested her head there.

'I'm quite a strong person,' she said. 'At least people always say I am, and they're probably right. I can be brave and even stoical. I can stand adversity, I believe, if it comes by itself. But I don't think,' she added quietly, 'I can take adversity and love at the same time.'

iv

A month after our return from Raasay, Haldane came back. He had been to Australia, he told Clarissa, and rather to his surprise he had found it a fine country. In fact he had decided to sell Dundallon, buy a farm in New South Wales and settle there with the family.

Three days after his arrival, Clarissa telephoned to ask me to supper.

'If you can think of some way of dissuading him from Australia, I would be grateful. But please be careful. He's suspicious about us.'

Haldane's appearance had changed over the previous two months. His face was ruddier, though it was not clear whether this had been caused by sun or drink or a combination of the two. He seemed heavier too, particularly around his eyes and neck. And he had abandoned tweeds and a tie for a khaki safari jacket and an open-neck shirt.

'I hear you've been holidaying with my wife,' he said

150

in that familiar tone which comprised jest and aggression in equal measure.

'Someone had to. And as you seemed reluctant yourself . . . .'

'Well, I wouldn't have chosen you, even though you are her cousin. I wouldn't trust you with the housekeeper. Anyway, what do you want to drink?'

'I'd like some whisky. With water.'

He poured two large glasses but added no water to his own.

'Don't look so censoriously at my drink. Clarissa tells me you were drinking flagons of the stuff in Raasay. You even converted her to island malts.'

At supper in the kitchen he talked about Australia.

'I'm hoping to buy this farm. It's a wonderful place, about three hours north-west of Sydney. Good house, lush fields, no problem with water, and it's already well-stocked. It just needs a couple of years' careful management and it will produce a decent income. Have you ever been to Australia?'

'No.'

'I expect you've got a snooty, typically British attitude about it. Think it's all convicts and kangaroos and dumb gum-chewers in the outback. Well it's not like that, not at all. It's a great country with plenty of elbow room. You can breathe out there. And, unlike this place, it's got a future.'

'Since when have you thought Britain had no future?' asked Clarissa.

'When you go to a place like Australia, it really strikes you how much we've lost the spirit of enterprise. And I doubt we'll get it back, even with this government.'

'Who was it,' Clarissa asked no one in particular, 'whose one ambition in life was to visit every country in the world except Australia?'

'Well there you are, that says everything. A stuck-up Englishman so prejudiced he decides it's awful without going there. It's ridiculous to be chained to stereotypes. Australia's a young country, it's started a good film industry, it's producing fine writers.'

'Who live in London,' I said.

'What the hell do you know about it?'

'I merely said that some of their writers live in London. I know, because I've met them.'

'A few exiles perhaps, but most of them work in Australia.'

'And you're going to invite them all to the farm . . .' began Clarissa.

'What?'

'. . . Like you do here. All those intellectual dinner parties you host for Glasgow's best writers.'

Haldane frowned and reached for the whisky bottle.

'What are you talking about?' he asked testily.

'I mean, what's the advantage of being near writers if you don't see them or read their books?'

Her husband pushed his chair back noisily and glared at her and then at me.

'What's this then, a conspiracy? First you seduce my wife, then you plot to wreck my future. . . .'

'He hasn't seduced me. Don't be ridiculous.'

'There's no plot,' I said, attempting to speak calmly. 'I just think you're trying to do everything in too much of a hurry. You love Dundallon and you always have. Naturally, Britain has gone rather sour for you now, but it will change. And anyway, why rush into something you may regret? You could always spend some time in Australia, make sure you really like the country before selling up and emigrating.'

'You mean I should go back now so you and Clarissa can go on sleeping together?'

'Oh for God's sake, I'm only trying to help.'

'It's a funny way of helping people,' he muttered, 'going to bed with their wives.'

I went to London the next day and a week passed before I saw Clarissa again.

'How is he?' I asked after we had met at the old curling pond, midway between Dundallon and Starne.

'One good thing's happened. That wretched farm in Australia has been sold privately, so it's no longer a threat.'

'Presumably there are others.'

'Yes, but he hasn't seen them. And at the moment he seems to have lost interest. He's become apathetic.'

'Would you have gone with him?'

'I don't know. Probably. I tried not to think about it. I didn't want to think of the future at all. I still don't. When things go well, you want to think of the future all the time, plan for next year and the next holidays. And when they go badly, you don't want to think of it at all, because you know each possibility is worse than the other. Do we have a future? No. Do I have a future with Roddy? I don't know. I don't even know if I want one.'

We walked up the lane lined by diseased elms, already half-leaved, withering in youth, and then we reached the hills and looked down at the plain, at the long stubbled fields which seemed like giant doormats spread out in the sun. I too didn't want to think of the future. Life consisted of hanging on, of not letting things get worse; negative hopes – don't let's break up, don't go to Australia – but nothing positive because there was nothing positive to hope for. Neither of us enjoyed that existence – the occasional walk, the occasional lunch, the rare opportunity for love – but it was better than the alternative, and better probably than a monstrous upheaval.

'But otherwise he's no better. In fact worse. He's

convinced we are having an affair and he goes on and on about it, every evening, getting nastier and nastier as he becomes drunker. I tell him we are close cousins but he dismisses it. He says cousins can have affairs just like anybody else and talks about all the royal marriages in history that have been between first cousins.'

'But why does he think we're having an affair now instead of last year when I spent more time at Dundallon?'

'I expect that's my fault. Since he came back I have felt repelled by him. I can't bear to have him near me. We made love once but it was awful and since then I've refused him.'

She gripped my arm and said forcefully with sudden anger: 'I am naturally monogamous, it's not like with you. I am naturally faithful. And I want to be faithful to you now, not to him. I hate letting him touch me.'

We had reached the ruined abbey on the edge of the Starne park, those old ivy-draped stones which had lain there since England's last King Henry had sent Lord Hertford north for the Rough Wooing: Melrose, Jedburgh, Holyrood, Starne – the smoking abbeys that had been the tyrant's vengeance for his failure to win our queen for his son. A part of the refectory had been less damaged than the rest and my grandfather had repaired it to use for winter shooting lunches. I remembered the great fire and the benches and the trestle tables, and Clarissa and her sister handing bowls of soup to the shooting guests.

We came quite often to that place now, to lie among the wild flowers and the mossed-over walls. It had a sense of peace which had prevailed in spite of the monster who had destroyed the monastic civilization of England and then ordered his generals to pillage ours. If I had achieved nothing else, I had at least prevented it from being turned into the club house of a projected golf course.

'I don't know how long all this can go on,' she said sadly. 'Something's got to end but I don't know what. And whatever it is, I know I can't make the decision to end it.'

She lay quietly for a while, her head on my chest, while I stroked her chestnut hair.

'There's only one time of the day I look forward to,' she said at last, 'apart from the days when we can actually meet. And it's right at the end, after everything. After I've driven the boys to and from nursery school, after I've done the shopping, after I've cooked several meals, after I've watched Roddy stagger up to bed having finished his daily bottle of whisky; then I have some time of my own. And I wait for him to fall asleep before going up and creeping into my side of the bed. I lie there, trying to stay awake, clutching the spare pillow and reliving the times we have been together in Raasay and since. I go to sleep imagining we are making love and I wake up thinking of you beside me.'

Chapter Six

i

I now dreaded the weekly suppers for the three of us at Dundallon. But I went on going to them because Clarissa begged me to. It was a relief for her, she said, and it also seemed more normal if we carried on as before. Within a month of his return, Haldane had become so slumped and torpid that I almost felt guilty I had helped dissuade him from going to Australia. He still drank tumblers of whisky so dark they looked like helpings of maple syrup. And he still sarcastically disagreed with anything I said. It was impossible to make even a sympathetic enquiry without provoking a sneering response.

Each time he made some reference to our affair, but he never looked for evidence and I don't know whether he really believed we were lovers. He simply asserted the fact and accused us both of disloyalty.

'It's a bloody poor show to sleep with the wife of your oldest friend isn't it? Bad form I'd say, bloody bad form.'

Then one night he said something he must have been tempted to reveal each time he saw me. He was even drunker than usual, and when he began to wag his finger at me, his elbow slipped off the table and he had to start again.

'I may be a failure,' he said deliberately, 'and I may be a cuckold, but at least I can say that my heir is my own child.'

'Of course he is,' said Clarissa quickly. 'What an absurd thing to say. Nobody's ever doubted it. Would you like some more wine, Hugh?'

Haldane was still staring at me and suddenly I understood what he was trying to say.

'Mine,' he said, pointing to his chest and belching disgustingly. 'No bastards in my house.'

'Roddy darling, you do say the most pointless things. Nobody's ever suggested they're not your sons: unfortunately they all look exactly like you.' She glanced at her watch and said, 'My goodness it's late. I think we really ought to go to bed. I've got to get up in the morning.'

'Yes,' said Haldane getting laboriously to his feet and belching again, 'I think I need a bit of shut-eye.'

As he lurched towards the stairs, Clarissa whispered, 'Would you like to stay for a while? We could play one of the Brahms. Which would you like?'

We went into the drawing room but I did not go to the piano. I felt a strange tingling sensation which began in my brain, descended to my stomach and then out into my limbs.

'What's the matter?' she asked as I sat heavily on the fireplace fender. 'Do you want a glass of water?'

'Is it true?' I asked slowly.

'Is what true?'

'What your husband implied.'

'He wasn't implying anything. He was far too drunk. He seemed to be talking complete nonsense.'

I grasped one of her wrists and pulled her towards me.

'Clarissa, please don't lie, even if you're trying to protect me. I love you. You are the most important person in the world to me, and therefore you of all people must tell me

157

the truth. Is it true what he implied – that Stephen is not my child?'

She gave a long sigh and sat beside me on the fender.

'I don't know. Some people seem to think so.'

'You mean it's a rumour?'

'Yes.'

'And like every rumour about sex, everyone mentions it every time my name comes up.'

'No, that's not true.'

'All right, not every time, because they know it already. But would you say that most people – those for example who come to your dinner parties – had heard it?'

'I expect some of them have. But after all it is only a rumour. Nobody knows. It's one of those "they say" rumours which everybody mistrusts, something someone probably told someone else in London which eventually found its way up here. I don't suppose it's much comfort but if anyone asks me I always say it's not true.'

'And how are you supposed to know?'

'I don't know. Nobody asks that.'

I sat on, unable to grasp the situation. A voice in my brain said: 'Don't you realize what has happened? Don't you see that your life is in ruins?' But I didn't see. They could have been questions asked of someone else.

'It doesn't make much difference,' I said at last, 'but do you know whose child he's supposed to be?'

Clarissa gulped, perhaps with embarrassment. 'There was a rumour it might have been a Portuguese communist.'

I tried to recall the wandering revolutionaries who used to drop in at the flat. I remembered communists from half-a-dozen other countries before I could picture the Portuguese Stalinist.

'Yes, I remember him now. Mario I think he was called. A short fanatic with a beard, dark-skinned, glinting eyes. It would explain why Stephen is darker than the girl.'

'It may not. Beatrice is darker than me and it doesn't mean a thing. The rumour may be totally untrue. He could easily be your son.'

'He's not.'

'How do you know?'

'I just do, I can feel it. It's obvious now when I remember what she was like at the end of her pregnancy. She was flustered and uneasy.'

'What will you do if you're right?'

'Ellen's coming up on Friday. I'll ask her about it and then decide.'

She sighed. 'I wish that fool Roddy hadn't been so drunk.'

'No, it's better to know now. It would be worse to find out in twenty years' time.' I paused and took her hand. 'It was good of you not to tell me before. You must have been tempted to.'

She led me to the front door and kissed me goodbye.

'I'll ring you tomorrow. No, I'll come to see you. But promise me not to do anything silly.'

I drove back through the rain to Starne and went into the red drawing room. There was a full bottle of brandy on the drinks tray and I poured myself a large glass. I sat in an armchair and drank it fast, unable still to understand fully the nature of the crisis. It was the sort of thing that destroyed other people's lives, not mine, and perhaps I drank so much to delay the realization of that truth.

There was a soft noise behind me and I looked around. No one was there and for a while I could see no evidence for the sound. Then I saw on the carpet a cluster of petals. One of the autumn roses from a vase arranged by Mrs Ross had dropped all at once and the petals lay scattered on the floor, some withered, the colour of parchment, the rest a perfect ivory. I gathered them up and smelt them; they still retained the freshness of smell and the suppleness of texture.

I took another glass of brandy to bed and began to read from my grandfather's bible which I kept on the bedside table. I read for a time without comprehension and then went to the medicine cupboard to search for sleeping pills. Failing to find them, I returned to the drawing room to fetch the brandy bottle and then lay in bed trying to make myself sleepy on Herod and the flight into Egypt. The storm grew worse, the rain splattering the window panes, the wind bellowing down the chimneys, and eventually it caused a power cut which forced me to abandon the gospel. I sat drinking in the dark and at about six I dozed for a few minutes before waking with the same sensation, sharp but empty in my stomach.

I tried to convince myself that it did not really matter. It was a mistake, it could have happened to anyone; it undoubtedly had happened to many people. In any case it was the person who mattered, the being, the character whom you saw moulded and brought up, not the germ-cells of the fertilizing semen. But whenever I thought of Mario, this argument disintegrated. Was I really obliged to bring up the son of a Portuguese Stalinist in my house, in my ancestor's house, to allow him to dispose of the inheritance of a family with which he was unconnected? Moreover, it couldn't be done secretly, with some concession to family pride, because everyone knew about it. All those inane friends of Haldane's – Harrington, Arbuthnot, his wife who thought Chopin was a nightingale – all of them had laughed at me. Doubtless many others had as well. I wondered about Logan and Bill Lindsay and the Hoggetts. Did everyone at Starne know: Mrs Ross, Wee Hovis, even the boy's nanny? Yes, no doubt, this type of gossip invariably broke records. Everyone was sniggering at me, the cuckold, the fool with the horns, the oldest figure of fun in the human book.

I got up, had a bath and went down to the kitchen for a cup of coffee. I could not bear to see the children so I left a note for Maggie saying I had to go out early. From my study I telephoned the doctor's surgery to make an appointment, but our doctor was away and I had to see someone else. It was awkward, asking for sleeping pills and tranquillizers because the strange doctor wanted to know why I needed them.

'You can ask Dr Richardson about me. He knows me well and knows I am not a crackpot who's going to take an overdose. It's simply that a combination of work and other problems have coincided at a difficult moment and they keep me awake and worried.'

The doctor raised an eyebrow but agreed to write out the prescription.

'Remember not to take the tranquillizers before driving.'

I drove towards home and then realized that I could not face Starne and its people and my ancestors on the walls. So I turned the car around and went west, driving for hours before I reached the hills and glens of Ravensmuir. I didn't want to see the house, gutted by the fire and restored recently by a hotelier, but I wanted to be in that country, Lochinvar's country, with the cloud shadows on the moors and the sun glisking on the scores of hillside burns erupting after the night's storm.

I parked by the wall of the kitchen garden and walked through the forlorn autumn fields with their blond grass and dying thistles and black Galloway cattle. A small group of rams, their horns extravagantly curled, watched me as I marched past. There were hips in the hedges and bright clusters of rowan berries. The ash was already leafless, the broom heavy with seed pods, dark and

161

somewhat sinister. I closed the gate on the last field and then I was on the hillside, walking through the ginger-coloured bracken. All around me were the hills of my childhood, the great rounded hills which seemed like venerable armchairs, their deep folds reminding me of an old velvet cushion someone had sat on.

I walked to the head of the glen and then arbitrarily to places I did not recognize. I left the sheep and the black cows behind and stumbled upwards, across rocks and peat bogs, up a hillside so steep that the easiest ascent was by the stones of a running burn. The mists were coming down on the other side of the glen but I would not have cared if they had swept across and enveloped me. I reached the top, disturbing a brace of grouse, and then the mists did come down and my sense of direction failed me. I wanted to be lost and to be forced to think of survival, because then I would not have to debate matters of shame and pride and humiliation. But I never could be lost in those hills for there were always the burns, and even if these did sometimes lead to the edge of a cliff, there was invariably a way down nearby and you only had to follow the water as it drained to the long valley and the sea.

This frenetic wandering achieved nothing of course. It did not help me to think rationally, to consider whether I could accept the fact, to plan what I should say to Ellen when she arrived the next day. It only encouraged me to rage against the humiliation, to shout to the winds that I had been betrayed and made ridiculous by my wife. How could she have done that, I cried, after I had given her so much? I had made so few demands, asserted such negligible claims, allowed so much independence, and in return she had made a fool of me and scoffed at my family. Yet it was a mistake, I kept reminding myself, not a planned humiliation. Was I not behaving like Browning's Ferrara, all pride and rigidity, complaining because my wife had regarded a centuries-old name as no gift at all?

Clarissa was sitting in the drawing room when I returned, looking at an old photograph book.

'I've been so anxious about you. Where have you been?'

'I went to Ravensmuir.'

'To Ravensmuir? Why? You should have taken me. I haven't been there since it was burnt down. How are you?' she enquired in a different tone.

'All right.'

'I telephoned a dozen times and then I drove around. Mrs Ross said she was sure you'd be back this evening, so I came in here and lit a fire. It was arctic.'

'Yes. Shall we have a drink?' I went over to the drinks tray and noticed that the half-empty brandy bottle had been returned from my bedroom. Mrs Ross must have been horrified on finding it.

'What are you doing?' I asked.

'I've been looking at the photograph book which Granny did for you. Finding pictures of you and me as children. Look at us here, after church on Christmas Day, Beatrice and me in muffs and fur hats, you in a tam o'shanter.'

I took the book and turned the stiff white pages. I guessed that Clarissa had not been searching for pictures of us together but trying to see if there was any resemblance between me and Stephen. I looked at photographs of my fifth year, in kilts and duffle coats and my grandfather's cricket cap, on a camel at the zoo, with Nanny pushing my brother in his pram; in one, sitting on a lilo pretending to smoke my father's pipe, I looked very like Lucy.

'You can see there's no connection,' I said at last. 'And why should there be? How could one expect a boy with Jewish-Portuguese parents to look like an Anglo-Scot?'

'Were you never suspicious before?'

'No, amazingly enough. It's been a pretty odd and unsatisfactory marriage. But it had a code, and honesty was an important part of it. If she wanted to have the second child, why didn't she leave? What was the point of carrying on with me?'

Clarissa stirred the fire with the poker and put on more logs.

'Have you decided yet what you're going to do?'

'No, I've no idea. She's coming tomorrow and I haven't decided anything. Every time I think about it, I change my mind. What do you think I should do?'

'I think,' said Clarissa, who had no doubt anticipated the question, 'it would be a very fine thing to accept the situation and to forgive her. But I also think it would be very difficult, especially for a man.' She paused and sipped her drink. 'And it would be particularly difficult in these circumstances, Stephen being the heir and the only boy. However liberated we may think we are, these things still matter. Inheritance and primogeniture – carrying on the line and all the rest of it – have been with us for thousands of years. They're one of the main impulses of human action. The men who went out to conquer kingdoms did not do it only for themselves but to found a dynasty and acquire some kind of immortality. Like the people who spent decades building great houses and died before they were finished. Our generation may despise all this but it cannot cancel out five thousand years of history.'

I felt I might have been able to forgive Ellen if I had liked her better. But in recent years we had lost most of our old affection for each other. She had begun to irritate me a long time before, long before I found that I loved Clarissa, and now I was happier when we were apart. I was bored by her politics and her feminism and her endless theories of imperialist plots. Her current obsession with nuclear disarmament and the 'Peace Movement' was particularly tiresome because of the smugness with which she assumed infallibility and treated those who disagreed as if we were members of a sort of 'War Movement'.

'If it had been you,' I told Clarissa, 'I might have been able to forgive. But not Ellen. I don't want to, even if it means losing the girl. I just don't want to be with her.'

She shook her head.

'You wouldn't have been able to forgive me either, even if you had wished to. There would always be resentment, always a feeling of humiliation. It's a problem of pride. Especially male pride,' she added with a smile.

ii

'You're looking a wee bit peaky,' said the factor as I entered the estate office next morning. 'Are you not feeling so well?'

'I'm fine. Slept badly, that's all.'

'We missed you at the committee last night.'

'What committee? Oh yes, the horticultural society. I am sorry, I forgot all about it.'

'No bother,' said Logan, folding up his copy of the *East Lothian Courier*. 'I took the chair myself.'

'Did anything interesting happen?'

'We had a fine tussle right enough. You should have seen the passions burning among the gentle ladies of the district. Oh my! The society is split, nay riven from head to foot, between those who wish to reduce the dahlia class to four blooms and those who will have heart failure unless it remains at five.'

'And which way did you cast the Starne vote?'

'As befitted the chairman and arbitrator of the proceedings, I remained aloof. I believe at one stage I essayed a compromise, four and a half said I, but they didn't see the joke. Mrs Boyd remarked severely that we were discussing matters of import.'

I yawned and looked through the day's mail. The sleeping pills had put me to sleep but not for long, and I had woken early after absurd dreams. I had dreamt that I was dying and that my only chance of survival was to regain consciousness. So I struggled in my sleep until I did wake and even then, when I was fully conscious, I was sure I would have died if I had stayed asleep. I had remained awake for several hours afterwards, trying to work out what I would say to Ellen. I rehearsed several conversations and rejected them all. I did not know what I ought to do or what I wanted to do. The simplest solution would be to sell everything, migrate to a different continent and start again – just as I had advised Haldane not to do.

'Did you hear about Mrs Graham?' Logan broke in.

'No.'

'The poor lady came to me in tears yesterday afternoon. Her golden retriever, a lovely dog it was, had been shot by our friend Hoggett.'

'I don't believe it!'

'God's truth.' He held up his hand. 'It got into one of the fields at Abbey Mains and cornered some sheep. Didn't touch them, mind you, wasn't going to harm them. But that wee bugger went for his gun. If you ask me, it's his revenge for the pony paddock.'

'What did she want you to do?'

'Just commiserate, I expect. But I was angry enough to go round and remonstrate and ask him to apologize. And do you know what he did? He lost his temper and said she should apologize to him for causing the trouble! Sometimes I think he's not a human being.'

Logan handed me a sheaf of estimates and the draft of a new tenancy agreement. I glanced through them, bored more than ever by details of administration.

'What's this?' I asked, holding up an almost illegible sheet of handwriting.

'That's the estimate for cleaning the Mortlake tapestries.'

'I didn't know one cleaned tapestries.'

'I believe it should be done once in each generation. Mr Kirkpatrick approached Mrs Ross about it a week ago, saying he had last cleaned them in 1955. Apparently he puts them into a huge trough, adds a mild detergent and then walks over them with sponges on his boots. Aye,' he grinned, 'we live in a scientific age.'

I approved the estimate and told him I would think about the others.

'And now I need some fresh air,' I said pushing my chair back. 'I'll go and see how those Kelso foresters are getting on.'

I crossed the garden and found Wee Hovis in the herbaceous border. He was looking up at the sky, watching a long jagged line of geese flying south from the Forth.

'I hate to see those creatures now,' he said, leaning on his spade. 'It makes one realize winter's nearly on us.' Then he smiled and added wistfully, 'It's all right when they're going the other way.'

'I heard you had a bit of trouble at the horticultural committee. I'm sorry I wasn't there.'

The gardener slapped the spade handle in disgust. 'It's a scandal,' he declared. 'Anyone can grow a dahlia with four blooms by the end of August.'

Even Wee Hovis, the kindest man in the district, shared the East Coast narrow-mindedness. How could I get on with people who worried about the dahlia competition at a village horticultural show? I blamed both myself and them for this failure of understanding, but it was nobody's fault. It was the fault of my upbringing and education. Once I had belonged to Starne, but I had been taken away, educated elsewhere and brought up in such a way that I no longer belonged. I had misunderstood the country from the beginning, going to live in the north as a Labour voter naturally sympathetic to the Scottish working class. Yet I found there not the lined hungry faces of Maxton's Clydeside supporters but the surly fleshy expressions of people who could afford to grow beer-bellies on the dole. We never understood each other and therefore we could never talk properly. Our conversations were courteous but predictable: about the weather, about the past, about the failures or disasters which had afflicted someone in the neighbourhood. But there was no genuine communication.

My problem of 'belonging' applied not only to the community but also to the countryside. I loved the smells and views of the landscape, but I did not love its ways or its uses. In London I had thought of the country as the place of life, where 'real' living took place. It was only when I lived there that I understood it was in reality a place of death; not just accidental deaths, dead hares on the roads and sheep's carcasses in the hills, but organized death – execution was a better word – the deaths of creatures that got in the human way, like the crows whose corpses hung along fence wires in hideous black rows. 'Vermin', a word we applied to certain birds and animals to prevent us feeling pity for them, were killed so that pheasants could be bred for us to kill as well. Butterflies and bees were killed by pesticides so that more corn could be grown for the animals we were going to eat.

It was ridiculous to think of the countryside as a

place of civilization because everything man did had the objective of killing and eating. Yet the greed and slaughter were little worse than the hypocrisy which often accompanied them. I was disgusted by people who could drool over a lamb which had lost its mother when the real aim was simply to fatten it up for the slaughterhouse. The same people became equally sentimental about a calf shipped abroad a few days after its birth so that the French could have the veal and the British could get at its mother's milk.

I walked through the park and sighed at the silhouette of the great elm, its dead branches standing out like veins against the dull autumn sky. The disease had taken hold quickly and the tree would soon have to be cut down. Or perhaps it would fall in one of the season's gales, in one of those storms people said came straight from Siberia. It would be an appropriate end, and it would be an appropriate end for us as well. Perhaps we were destined to go together, the great tree, planted by one of the first Gordons of Starne, and the family which no longer had any reason to be there, a family which had been dying slowly for a long time and had at last reached the end with a bastard as its heir.

When Ellen arrived in the late afternoon, I was still undecided about how to confront her. I had had a few drinks during the day and taken some tranquillizers. But I remained nervous and annoyed by my nervousness, because she was the guilty one and I was in the right. I should have asked her straight out, after she had seen the children. But I waited until we had had supper and gone along to the library. And then, with yet another brandy in my hand, I began obliquely, with a foolish question about Portugal.

'It's just another capitalist country,' replied Ellen, 'not interesting at all. The progressive forces are beaten, the farms are being given back to the landowners and that's all there is to it. I don't really follow it any more.'

'So you're not in touch with your old communist friends?'

'Not at all. But I never knew them that well anyway. Just a few guys around Octavio.'

'Wasn't there a journalist called Mario?'

'I don't remember. I don't think so.'

'Surely you remember him. One of Cunhal's men. Fellow with a beard.'

'Yeah, maybe there was a guy like that. I'd forgotten him.'

'I see. Do you forget all your lovers so easily?'

She was sitting crosslegged on the hearth rug, sorting various pamphlets from a large canvas bag.

'What's this,' she challenged, 'an inquisition?'

'I was merely asking about a lover.'

She raised her face and looked at me with narrowed angry eyes: the Red Indian look which I hated.

'According to our rules, it's no business of yours. I don't pry into your life. I don't ask if you're humping your secretary. I don't enquire what you're doing with your cousin. So you have no right to grill me about some guy in the past.'

'Those are indeed the rules. But the first rule of all is that we should never tell lies.'

'I haven't told any goddamn lies.'

'All right then. But I have to ask you one question about Mario. Is he Stephen's father?'

Her mouth dropped open and she swore. 'Oh Jesus! Of course he's not. I hardly knew the guy.'

'You promise he wasn't a lover?'

'Okay, maybe I did screw him a couple of times, but so what? It wasn't important.'

'Once is enough.'

'Don't be so goddamn obvious.'

'You swear it's not true.'

'Yes I do.'

'Can you explain then why people up here think he is the father?'

'What people? Your cousin I suppose. Right, I see it now. Trying to dump that asshole of a husband. He was grand enough when he was in the government, but now he's just a wino loser and she wants something better. So what does she do? Opens her legs for her cousin, tells him lies about his wife and wow! there we go. Queen Clarissa. Countess of Starne. What a trip!'

'As a matter of fact Clarissa didn't tell me. She even tried to persuade me it wasn't true.'

'You can't deny she's screwing you.'

'I don't deny it. But she's not trying to break up either our marriage or her own.'

'That's what you think. You were never too bright about female psychology.'

'Look, Clarissa is irrelevant to this conversation. We are talking about Stephen and you and a Portuguese Stalinist called Mario. I asked you a question and I need to discover if you are telling me the truth. So tomorrow morning I shall take Stephen to the health centre for a blood test.'

'You can't prove paternity with blood tests.'

'That's true, they can't prove who is the father. But they can usually demonstrate who isn't. If Stephen and I don't have the same blood group. . . .

In any case they've developed some new thing called genetic fingerprinting. It's one hundred per cent accurate.'

'I see you've done your research.'

'Not at all, but I sometimes read the newspapers.'

We sat in silence in front of the library fireplace, both of us now drinking brandy.

'I'm not bluffing,' I said at last. 'I've already made the appointment.'

Ellen raised her chin and for the first time I saw in her face guilt and fear as well as defiance.

'Okay,' she said flatly, 'it was Mario.'

She closed her eyes and exhaled a long sigh. There was no noise but for the irregular ticking of smouldering logs.

'I know it's not much use trying to say sorry,' she said gently. 'But I am. I have been since it happened. I made a terrible mistake, a ridiculous miscalculation with my dates. And when I realized the mistake, it was too late. I was seven months' pregnant.'

She talked without looking me in the eyes, picking bits of fluff from the rug and throwing them into the fire.

'It was only later when I looked in my diary that I knew I had been careless. I'd thought it was a safe period but I was a week out. I panicked and consulted a gynaecologist who looked at the dates and said it could have been either of you. If I had ovulated early it would have been his, if late it would have been yours. I thought about it all the time and hoped to God I had ovulated late. And then, after the birth, the first thing I did when they gave me the child was to look at his face to see whose features he had. I couldn't tell of course, he didn't look human. But I knew instinctively that Mario was the father. Since then I have felt terrible about it, I have honestly, and several times I nearly told you. But I thought maybe it was better to say nothing and hope no one found out. It was because I felt guilty that we kind of drifted apart. I'm not completely heartless. I didn't want you to love me after I had betrayed you.'

'And why did people find out?'

'I don't know. I never told anyone.'

'Except Mario.'

'No, not even Mario. I didn't want him shooting his mouth off.'

'Someone must have known.'

'No one knew exactly, but I guess some people were suspicious. I remember a committee meeting when everyone was stoned and some guy was teasing me, saying it was a scandal I was about to give birth to a feudalist oppressor. And another guy said it was more likely to be a Portuguese commie and everyone laughed and Mario went crimson.'

'So they all knew you were sleeping with him?'

'Yes.'

'And it wasn't only twice?'

'No.'

'And now everyone's laughing about it up here. I wonder what route it took from your committee guerrillas to the Scottish gentry.'

'Men always think everyone finds it hilarious when their wives deceive them. But it's not true.'

'It is true. It's the theme of half the world's comedies.'

Ellen attempted no tears, no embraces, no pleas for forgiveness. I was relieved by that and impressed. I think it made me feel less angry than I expected. But lying awake in the early morning I became angry again at the thought of the sniggering and the ridicule. What right had that absurd man Harrington to laugh at me? Yet the people who did not know might be even more unbearable. How could I listen to someone who claimed to see a resemblance between Stephen's ears or fingers and my own? What could I reply to anyone who said he had my mother's laughter or held a cricket bat like my grandfather?

An art historian arrived in the afternoon to look at some of the pictures. As he was particularly interested in Lawrence, I took him up to the gallery above the inner

173

hall and showed him the portrait of the admiral and his wife. The arrogant naval officer stared down at me with disapproval, as if he had always known I would fail the family. I turned to the other ancestors but they also seemed to have known. The face of the governor-general was contorted by contempt.

'You can see,' remarked the historian looking at me with a smile, 'that the family resemblance lives on.'

I suddenly felt faint and grasped the banisters. I closed my eyes, imagining the house in the future, open to the public, a guide taking a party of tourists around the gallery. She stops at the portrait of myself and says, 'This is the eleventh earl, one of the least interesting members of the family. He achieved nothing noteworthy in his life.' And then she points to Stephen's dark Mediterranean features in the picture next to it. 'With the twelfth earl you can see that the family resemblance comes to an end. Officially this was ascribed to the strong genes of his American mother, but I am sure you are all aware that the real father [snigger, snigger from the tourists] was a member of the Portuguese Communist Party.'

In that house I had never been able to escape from my ancestors, but now it was worse. They followed me along the passages and into all the rooms, they pursued me out of doors and persecuted me with their works. They prevented rational thought, their presence insisting that the 'scion' had betrayed the family and consigned it to history. In my anger and frustration I turned on Ellen, determined to punish her for my humiliation. I talked sarcastically about her carelessness and her deceit.

'I never asked much of you. I didn't search for clues in your handbag. I never rang you at three in the morning. The only thing I expected was that you would be discreet. But you couldn't be. You're too selfish for that. If it didn't matter to you, then it didn't matter full stop. That's your creed, isn't it? And stuff everybody else and their feelings too.'

'For Christ's sake, it was a mistake.'

'I know it was. You couldn't be bothered to put in your Dutch cap. Probably you were too stoned to remember when you'd had your last period. Or perhaps you were busy thinking of some solidarity meeting. Solidarity comes first always. Ruining other people's lives is comparatively unimportant.'

'Don't be so obnoxious. If you can't talk rationally, there's no point discussing it.'

'Of course there's no point. I talk like this because I'm angry. Nobody could be rational in this situation.'

'You could, but you don't try. You're just obsessed with your stupid family and the past. Why not think about the present? A week ago you called me and said Stephen was a great kid. Well he hasn't changed, he's still a great kid, only now you can't stand the sight of him.'

'You don't understand a thing, do you? You can't see that history and tradition and human impulses stop one being rational. You and your cronies are so certain you have all the answers that history becomes irrelevant, something to be scoffed at or bored by at school. You accuse me of double standards but civilization has always had double standards. If society's basic social unit was the family, then obviously women's infidelity was more dangerous than men's because it threatened family life. It was unfair, I agree, but it was logical. It's why the first civilized people, the Sumerians, punished female adultery and not male. And for seven thousand years each succeeding civilization has taken a similar view. It's a natural human instinct to want to raise your own children and not cuckoos, and it remains a natural instinct even in this age. Twenty years of the pill and a generation of feminist claptrap don't change human nature.'

For three days we went on like this. I began row after row, each time saying much the same things in much the same way. I became nastier and more brutal when drunk, but there was little other variation in our quarrels. We were unable to talk calmly about the future.

On the fourth afternoon of her visit Ellen told Maggie to pack suitcases for the children.

'Where are you going?' I demanded. 'You can't take them to the flat.'

'No, I'm taking them to New York to stay with my parents.'

'But it's the middle of term.'

'The children are four and six. They are not going to suffer from missing a few weeks of school. And if you're worried about what people are going to say, you can explain that their American grandfather is ill and wants to see the children before he dies.'

I sat down on the dressing-table stool and watched her pull clothes out of her wardrobe.

'Will you go for long?'

'I have no idea. Let's wait and see. I'm sure the best solution is to be apart for a while so we can both think independently what we want to do. And let's not be dramatic now about separating or saying goodbye to the children as if you're never going to see them again. We'll keep the options open, okay?'

Chapter Seven

Ellen left with the children on the night of 5 November. As I drove them to Prestwick, the children counted the bonfires and the rockets in the skies. And when we arrived at the airport Stephen looked up and said, 'There's no moon tonight because the fireworks have killed it.'

Lucy was nervous about the aeroplane: 'I've got an itchy feeling in my tummy.'

'That's just butterflies,' I said.

'But Daddy, I haven't eaten any butterflies.'

I remembered the children's last remarks as I drove back through the night and I cried at the memory. I recalled other things they had said and done and I was so overcome that I was a danger on the roads. On being told they were going to America for two weeks, Lucy said she would count every day that went by until she got to fourteen when she would hug me again. On that last morning she drew a picture of herself with a red pencil and left it on the desk in my study.

Lucy and Clarissa were the only beings I loved in the world; I felt I could have lived happily with them without seeing other people. After she had gone I wrote down as many things about my child as I could remember. I noted the things she had said, the places we had gone to, the little duets we used to play on the piano. I tried to describe how she, as a six year old, had converted me to vegetarianism. At the age of five she had asked why people needed to kill birds and animals, and shortly afterwards she had refused to eat meat. When she saw a poussin on my plate, she asked with a dismayed look if it had been born so that I could eat it. I can't remember what I said, but I thought to myself that it had indeed been bred and raised for my solitary pleasure. Later I had taken her to the dairy and the farmer's wife had shown her the new brown and white Ayrshire calves. Why weren't they allowed to stay with their mothers? Lucy had asked, and the woman had given her an unsentimental explanation of the economics of dairy farming. After that I too stopped eating meat.

Ellen and I had agreed we would preserve all options, but I think we both knew we would never live together again. I wanted desperately to live with Lucy, I could have lived with Stephen away from Starne, but I didn't want to be near Ellen. I never wanted to see her again.

I too went away, leaving Logan in charge of the estate and Mrs Ross in possession of the house. It seemed unlikely that I would live at Starne in the future, but I wanted to wait a little before deciding how to be rid of it. I needed to find something to do, a way of redeeming a wasted life, and a place which I could perhaps improve with money I received from the sale of my inheritance. I thought of going to the Caribbean to see my mother but I knew such a visit would not help. For years our relationship had consisted of nothing more than birthday cards and an annual telephone call at Christmas. She had come to London once, before we moved to Scotland, and met the children. But she had not come for my father's funeral; and I had never been to Jamaica to meet her second husband. I could not go there now, tell her how I had crashed my life and try to recreate the relationship of twenty-six years ago when she had sat on the edge of my bed and made me promise to love her always.

In the end I travelled in North Africa and the Middle East, meeting friends of friends in one country and then their friends and relations in the next. And eventually I came to a place on the edge of the desert where a large friendly doctor ran a school for refugees. He needed money for buildings and equipment and more teachers, but his chief backer had died and he doubted whether he could continue his work. One evening, as we drank a bottle of arak between us, he told me of his difficulties and suddenly I realized that we could solve each other's problems. I offered myself as a partner and a teacher of English and he stood up and embraced me and said we were brothers.

I stayed abroad for Christmas and New Year and then I returned home and told Clarissa of my plans.

'I don't want you to go,' she said.

'You know I can't stay here. Not after everything that has happened.'

It was dusk as we walked by the loch, waiting for the geese to come in.

'Do you remember those winters when we could skate here?'

'Of course. It always seemed to snow just after it had frozen, so we had to sweep it away.'

'There were no geese then,' said Clarissa.

'No. They come now for the winter corn. The farmers want to shoot them.'

The geese started to fly in, lines of sixty or seventy bunching as they saw the water and then gliding down to the loch. As they arrived, the mallard flew off in pairs, circling the water and then setting off for the smaller ponds in the woods. Occasionally a pair of teal rushed by, swooping with noisy wing beats over the reeds, flashing in different directions in the way that made them so elusive to the guns.

'I wish you would come with me,' I said, putting an arm around her shoulder.

'And abandon my children?'

'You could bring them with you.'

She smiled and shook her head.

'You can't really expect their father to let them go to a refugee school instead of a British preparatory.'

'If I didn't go abroad but went to live in London, would you come with me then?'

She stood on tiptoe to give me a light kiss on the cheek.

'I do love you but I can't go with you. You know that. I can't betray the people who need me.'

'You wouldn't be betraying your husband. You'd be justified in leaving him.'

'Not now, not when he's beaten. Perhaps before.'

We watched shivering as another line of greylag came in, flying high into the stiff wind and drifting down, lit up for a moment by a gold band of light in the western sky and then lost before the dark mass of trees which bordered the far side of the loch.

'It's a wonderful noise,' said Clarissa. 'Geese on the wing.'

'Yes.'

We walked away, glove in glove, towards the house.

'I was wrong,' she said, 'to ask you not to go abroad. You should go, for your sake and also for mine. You must realize we can't go on like this, we must go back to being friends and cousins.'

'Oh, please don't talk like that. You know how depressed it makes me. I have nothing in my life now except you.'

'So you expect me just to carry on until the day you leave the country?'

'I don't know. Maybe I won't go after all.'

We returned home in silence and lit a fire in the library. 'I want to be with you,' she said over a glass of Skye whisky, 'live with you, work in that school with you. But as I can't do that, I want to stop now. I don't want anything else. I don't want to go on with this deceitful existence.'

'It's not deceitful. We are victims not villains. We didn't deserve to suffer and you don't have to make sacrifices for his sake now. You owe him nothing.'

'It's not for his sake, it's for our own. We've both got to rebuild our lives, separate lives, and we cannot do that while we are still lovers.'

I threw a log on to the fire and said, 'You can't change things just like that. You can't decide suddenly that from this moment we are only friends. I will still love you even if I can't see you.'

'Perhaps,' she said softly. 'But we must still try to change. There is no other solution.'

After she had gone, I stayed for a long time in the library without moving. I repeated to myself many times the thought, 'This is the end of everything, the end of all things.' I didn't doubt that it was the end of our affair, for it was impossible to see how it could go on; it had always been impossible to envisage a future. I wondered if it had been worth it, but that was an awful thought, a question not to be answered. I put it differently: would I have lived it again? I didn't know. How could one weigh the magic of certain moments against the many hours of anguish and guilt? Keeping up appearances had robbed us of many things. I had never spent a whole night with Clarissa, never woken up to find her breathing quietly against my shoulder; we had never made love at Dundallon and very seldom at Starne in case we were discovered. It had been largely an affair of moorland walks, sun and heather when we were lucky, more often drizzled winds and a ruined bothy. Sometimes we had gone to hotels on the outskirts of Edinburgh, dingy establishments with grumpy receptionists. Clarissa, who always wore dark glasses in case she was recognized, hated them. 'How can you insult me by bringing me to a place like this?' she had once asked, half-laughing, fingering nylon sheets in disgust.

She calculated that we used to have about ten hours, or six per cent, of each week together. Some of that time was spent with Haldane as well, some of the rest wasted by argument and bouts of despairing guilt. She used to denounce herself as self-indulgent, betraying her husband and ignoring her children for her own pleasure. You couldn't enjoy reading *Babar the Elephant*, she claimed, while you were an adulteress. You couldn't feel enthusiasm for anything except being with your lover.

Subtracting the time lost with Haldane and the time taken by guilt, we were left with five or six hours a week. There were other good times of course, times when we were apart but knew we were thinking of each other, times when we looked from different houses at the Bass Rock and knew the other was looking at the same view, times when we lay in different beds and imagined ourselves in each other's arms. And yet still there were only five or six real hours, hours that counted, hours that were the culmination of all thoughts and all ambition. They were few indeed, but surely they were worth the others, the wasted ones; it was the intensity that mattered not the number.

I turned the lights off and went into the drawing room. I could not play the Brahms sonatas: I swore I would never play or even listen to them again. But the nocturnes were nothing to do with Clarissa. I would play them now, all the ones I knew, and I would play them by candlelight and dedicate them to her.

It snowed towards midnight and when I paused I could hear the light touch of snowflakes on the window panes. And then I heard a noise that seemed to be hail, separate bursts splattering the glass and the astragals. But I realized it would not be hailing so I stood up and looked out at the whitening landscape. And there was Clarissa below, bareheaded and frantic, aiming her third handful of gravel.

I ran down to let her in.

'Lock the door,' she gasped as she entered, 'for God's sake lock the door.'

I turned the key and pushed the bolts and clasped her. 'My love, what's the matter?'

She was cold and wet and shivering. Underneath her overcoat she wore only a nightgown and gumboots. Her hair was tangled and damped by melting snowflakes.

'I thought I'd better not shout or ring the bell in case I woke Mrs Ross.'

'It wouldn't matter. But tell me what's happened. Come and sit by the fire in the library – I'll get it going again and bring you some dry clothes.'

A few minutes later I poured her a drink while she stood by the fireplace, changing into some clothes of Ellen's.

'He might be here any minute,' she said. 'What on earth are we going to do?'

'I don't know. Does he know you are here?'

'He'll guess.'

'Well, what do you want me to do?'

I gave her a drink and she crouched down by the resurgent embers.

'You mustn't let him in,' she breathed huskily. 'He could kill us.'

'But what's happened to him suddenly?'

'He's gone mad, completely mad. Drunk as well of course, and totally irrational.'

I looked at the ground-floor windows of the library. They were shuttered and barred. Haldane couldn't have entered even if he had tried to shoot the locks out.

'You're safe here, my love, he can't get in. Now tell me what happened.'

She gave a long shuddering sigh, gulped her drink and talked.

'It was horrible, I've never seen him like that before. He was vicious and out of control. The drunker he got, the more demented he became about our affair. When we went up to bed he said he was damned well going to enjoy his marital rights even if it meant raping me. I refused and he started to slap me, first on the face and then all over my body. I was so terrified I eventually agreed to let him.'

She stared into the fire as she talked, biting her bottom lip at the end of the sentences to prevent herself crying.

'But that wasn't enough for him. When he got into bed he started saying the most appalling things. He said he wasn't going where you had been all afternoon, that I probably hadn't washed since and similar horrible things. Of course I said we had been watching the geese on the loch and he laughed nastily and tried to make me turn over. The other was your territory now, he said, and he wanted something new. Then I realized what he was after and I began to fight. Of course he's very strong and he would obviously have won in the end. But he was also drunk and clumsy and when I bit him he was so surprised I was able to wriggle away and run. He came after me but I managed to lock a passage door between us and tore down the stairs. My burberry and boots were in the hall.

So were my car keys. I grabbed them and ran and here I am.'

She looked up and smiled slightly.

'But I can't think what's happened to him. The hall lights were on and as I drove away I saw him coming down the stairs. Perhaps he went to get a gun, but still he should have been here long ago.'

'I expect he cooled down after the running and the night air. Then he changed his mind and went back to bed.'

She shook her head. 'You didn't see what he was like. I am sure he came after me. He couldn't have got in through some back door or scullery window, could he? Maybe he's waiting for us in the dark.'

'There's no danger of that. Mrs Ross locks everything several times over. And anyway it's not his style, is it, skulking in a passage. He'd be more likely to barge in here and start a fight.'

'Or a massacre.'

'Of course not, you're being melodramatic. I bet he's gone back to bed.'

We finished our drinks and I put the fireguard in position.

'You must stay here tonight and in the morning I'll take you back to Dundallon and the three of us can have a rational and sober confrontation. In the meantime,' I added, putting an arm on her shoulders, 'you must stop worrying about it. You're going to take a sleeping pill and sleep in my bed, and you won't have to do anything you don't want to.'

But neither of us felt sleepy. We lay holding each other under the eiderdown without speaking and almost without moving. I gave silent kisses to her neck, her cheeks and her forehead, until at last she spoke.

'The things I said this afternoon.'

'Yes?'

'Can we suspend them? Or perhaps I mean just forget. I don't know. I don't know if I meant them then and I don't know if I mean them now. I just don't want to think about any of it.'

'Nor do I.'

She sighed. 'It's my fault, I'm always trying to analyse everything. You're different, you live for the moment, you never think about consequences. I don't usually like that way, it's selfish, but I want us both to be selfish tonight. Will you?'

'Of course.'

She moved across me and then whispered very gently in my ear, 'Love me then.'

'I do,' I whispered back, adjusting to her movements and her rhythm. 'You know I do. I always will. I've been faithful to you all these months since we began. Even when I was abroad I never slept with anyone.'

'I don't believe you.'

'I swear it's true.'

'But why?'

'Because I love you. And perhaps also because I wanted to do something decent, make some kind of sacrifice. Like giving up whisky for Lent,' I added with a laugh.

'And did no one try to seduce you?'

'Not really. Perhaps they were put off by my monkish aspect. There was one woman in Istanbul who tried and I nearly succumbed. But I didn't. I knew I would be thinking of you all the time.'

She became silent above me, concentrating, moving and breathing faster, waiting until she was ready before demanding that I finished with her. She was never satisfied unless we came together.

Afterwards she laid her head on my shoulder and faced away from me. 'I didn't take the sleeping pill you gave me,' she said between long breaths. 'I didn't want to sleep. I wanted to live one night.' She said it seriously but then I heard her giggle. 'And I'm not going to let you sleep either. Not tonight.'

She hardly spoke during the following hours except at the climactic moments when she never knew what she was saying. And I said nothing either except that I loved her. That night, uniquely, she initiated everything, behaving as if it were her last night on earth, a final act of defiance before facing judgement and retribution. It was as if she were trying to extract every drop of passion from the rest of her life and burn it in a single sacrificial flame.

At last we fell asleep, but it was only a brief slumber. We were woken by a thumping on the door and Clarissa, lying across my chest, gripped me by my shoulders and said desperately, 'It must be Roddy.'

Turning on the lamp, I called that I was coming and reached for my dressing gown. But the door opened and Machale entered. He was shaking with agitation.

'A terrible thing's happened, sir,' he stammered. 'A terrible accident.'

He stood in the doorway in his butler's suit, hardly able to get the words out.

'Mr Lindsay found him, sir, down by the bridge.'

He had been staring at me all this time, but now he looked past and saw Clarissa in the bed. His mouth fell open and his stammer became worse.

'May I speak to you in private, sir?'

Tying the cord of the dressing gown as I went, I took him down the passage and into a spare room. The old man was breathing noisily.

'Tell me what's happened.'

'It's Sir Roderick, sir. He's dead. He's had an accident in his car. According to Mr Lindsay, there are tyre marks all over the road. He must have skidded on the ice just before the bridge.'

'Has Bob Lindsay called for an ambulance?'

'Yes sir, he's doing that in the kitchen just now. And the police as well. But it won't be any good. Sir Roderick's been dead hours.'

'How does he know?'

'He's cold. Mr Lindsay opened the door and found him slumped over the wheel. Broken neck. Stone dead.'

'Did he say anything else?'

'How do you mean, sir?'

'Did Mr Lindsay say anything about Sir Roderick's appearance for example?'

'Well yes, sir. He said he was rather oddly dressed and on the passenger seat there was a loaded shotgun. Mr Lindsay couldn't understand what he was doing with a gun in a blizzard.'

'No, it's curious.'

I could see the old butler's brain working, adding up the evidence: one man's wife in another man's bed, a dead husband by the park gates, a double-barrelled 12-bore ready for use. He would soon solve the mystery.

'Machale,' I said, attempting to speak with quiet authority, 'no one must learn that Lady Haldane was in this house. Is that understood?'

'Yes sir, of course. I quite understand.'

'I will take her back to Dundallon by the lower road and hope she gets there before the police. Tell Mr Lindsay I will see him later.'

It was a quarter past seven. If we hurried, I thought I could get Clarissa home before the police called to announce her husband's death. That seemed crucial if we were to avoid the press and years of scandal-mongering.

The urgency made it easier to tell her. I went downstairs to fetch her coat and boots and then told her the news. She took it quietly, said 'Oh God' and then sat immobile on the bed with her face in her hands.

'My love, you must hurry. I have to get you back to Dundallon.'

She slowly pulled on one of her boots and said, 'It's all my fault.'

'Of course it's not, but we can talk about that later. Now we must go. Think what a field day the press will have if they discover you spent the night here. A baronet killed trying to murder his wife and her lover would be the scandal of the decade.'

Perhaps I was brutal because I could see how vital it was for her and her children that there was no scandal; for myself it no longer mattered. Yet perhaps I was callous because I did not care about Haldane's death. I had hated him for so long, both for his treatment of Clarissa and for what he had done to me, that his end could not produce immediate charitable regret. Later, no doubt, I would remember the old friendship and be sad, but now it seemed merely the right end to a ruined life.

I drove the long way round to avoid the wrecked car and reached Dundallon while it was still dark.

'We were probably having sex,' she said in a flat tone, 'while my husband was dying.'

'Nonsense, it was an instant death. It must have happened immediately after you arrived.'

'Could there be anything worse,' she said, as if she had not heard my reply, 'than sleeping with someone while your husband lies dead in a ditch?'

'You have no reason to feel guilty. You can't be blamed for running away from him last night. And it's not your fault that he drove drunkenly into the bridge on his way to kill us. Now please go into your house before they all discover you're not there. I'll come and see you later.'

I returned to Starne and spent the morning telling lies to the police. No, officer, I could not say what Sir Roderick was doing in a midnight blizzard near my house. Nor could I imagine why he was wearing pyjamas under his corduroys. No, I was unable to guess why he drove with a loaded shotgun at his side. Sir Roderick was an old friend of mine. We had never quarrelled.

It was useless, of course, and I had to retract most of it in the afternoon. The Haldanes' nanny had heard her employers shouting in the night; their gardener, who was letting his dog out, had seen them run out of the house and drive off in separate cars. Knowing this, Clarissa had told the police most of the truth, and the officer returned to ask if I would like to amend my statement. He was reasonably understanding.

'I comprehend your motives, sir. But perjury is perjury nevertheless.'

'Of course, officer, I'm extremely sorry.'

In the evening I drove back to Dundallon. Clarissa was in the sitting room with her mother and one of Haldane's sisters. They were making arrangements for the funeral. Beatrice came in to ask if anyone wanted a drink and I went out to help her fetch some bottles.

'How is she?' I asked.

'Bad. She keeps saying it's her fault.'

'That's ridiculous,' I said angrily. 'He brought the whole thing upon himself. From the beginning.'

She looked quizzically at me, one eyebrow raised as she cracked ice cubes into a bucket. I hadn't seen Beatrice for many years. She was a little taller than her sister, a little darker, and perhaps more obviously glamorous. But she was also harder and there was the disapproval in her mouth that reminded me of Aunt Pamela.

'I gather she was with you when it happened,' she said

with the Canadian twang she had picked up from her husband. 'That doesn't make her feel too good.'

'Clarissa feels guilty even when she's behaved well. Most people would have left him months ago. Not just because of the scandal but because of the way he behaved afterwards. He took everything out on her – his rage, his frustrations, everything. And she was completely innocent. I don't know why she stuck it.'

'Especially,' smiled Beatrice as she replaced the ice tray in the freezer, 'when you were offering her an alternative.'

'Oh, so she's told you that, has she?'

'Well, she sort of broke down and confessed. Told Mum also, which didn't go down well. She's never been one of your greatest admirers.'

Later Clarissa took me into the study and asked me to sit down. I tried to embrace her but she pushed me away.

'Please do what I say. I think I have the right to demand that.'

'Of course.'

'Last night was an aberration. Ghastly, wonderful, whatever adjective you care to use. But it was a once only. Do you understand?'

I said nothing.

'It's all over, it can never happen again. I think I should tell you that now.'

'Of course it's natural you should think like that at this moment.'

'It's not a question of thinking. I know it now and I want you to accept it. I have been crucified every day for the last five months. I am not prepared to be crucified for the rest of my life.'

I drove over to Dundallon each day that week, trying to help with arrangements for the funeral and various problems with Haldane's will. I also dealt with the journalists who were less percipient than I had feared.

The Haldanes' quarrel came out, of course, but the fact that Clarissa and I were cousins convinced them that Starne was the natural refuge for a persecuted wife. The gun and the rest of Haldane's behaviour were ascribed to his alcoholism and ruined career.

The day after the funeral, Clarissa came to Starne and found me in the inner hall looking through old visitors' books.

'Hello,' she said, 'what are you doing?'

'Trying to sort out a few things.'

She looked over my shoulder as I turned the pages of self-confident aristocratic signatures – Erroll, Elgin, Montrose, Zetland – single name flourishes of a vanished era.

'Only seventy years ago,' she murmured, 'and our grandfather was a young man. Yet it seems much longer, a different civilization.'

'The First World War changed everything.'

'I suppose so.'

'And yet I go on pretending that I am still a part of that age, that I still belong to that world of grandee scrawls.'

We went into the library and I opened the shutters. The January sun aimed powerful rays from its low winter site above the Lammermuir ridge.

'Have you decided when you're going?' she asked.

'Not yet. I was waiting to learn of your plans.'

'I shall go on living at Dundallon with my children.'

'That really is your decision?'

'Yes.'

She moved towards the marble fireplace and turned to face me.

'You do understand, don't you, why it can't be?'

'I understand why we can't be together in Scotland. But elsewhere, abroad . . .'

192

'Then you haven't understood at all. It's not just the gossip and the scandal I couldn't accept. It's far more than that, it's me. For you it would be different because you have no reason to be ashamed.'

'Neither have you. As I told you before, we are both victims, we shouldn't have to suffer.'

'I feel guilty and I am guilty; that is something I have to expiate by not being with you. Otherwise it would attack me every day of our lives together. It would ruin everything.'

There was no point in saying anything more: she had only come to say goodbye.

'You must surely see,' she continued, 'that I have a duty to stay at Dundallon. I must bring Roddy's sons up there. I must see that the eldest inherits it.'

More victims of these wretched houses: I remembered how Quevedo had described royal palaces as 'sepulchres of a living death'. Dundallon and Starne had become sepulchres for our generation, chaining us dutifully to the past and preventing us from leading real existences.

Clarissa left and the last real thing in my life went with her. I went back to the hall and put away the visitors' books. They too were part of the sepulchre, part of that implacable nostalgia which crippled me. The regrets for my childhood were bad enough, forcing me to make long journeys in search of lost moments, but how much stranger and more destructive was that nostalgia for a past I had never known.

We should have gone long ago, I thought, a useless class in a world we neither liked nor understood. Better to have extinguished ourselves in a brief period of consuming decadence – after the last waltz, the guttering candles, the empty bottles of port on the green baize card-tables, the florid figures sprawled in leather armchairs waiting for the dawn footmen to remove them.

Better to have disappeared in the carts of the Terror or to have danced ourselves to death under the gaze of an emperor with a death wish. Better by far to have gone quickly with a final, hopeless, absurd flourish of bravado than to survive slightly, complacent and useless, without style, without wisdom, even without comprehension.

I went out into the garden. It had thawed in the last days and there were few traces of snow left. I walked over to the walled garden and gripped the large reddish stones coated with moss and strands of ivy. The place still trapped me. When those stones had seemed eternally mine, I had never wanted to touch them. But now I knew I was going, I held on to them as though they had been my closest treasures.

I looked back at the great house, the classical kernel with its late Georgian extensions, solid, imposing, redundant. It should not go quietly and bureaucratically, I thought, its fate organized by documents and negotiation. It should go as we, its creators, should have gone, rapidly and without pity once its role was over. I would have liked to see it consumed by a devastating fire, a flaming torch thrown on a gale night taking hold of the panelling and sweeping through the house. I thought sympathetically of Nero and his fiddle; I would have played my nocturnes during the Blitz. I thought of the Vandals in the Forum who destroyed civilized life for centuries and yet left the greatest ruins of all time. I wanted Starne to suffer like that. I wanted the house to die quickly and irrevocably, to die a death incapable of resurrection, a death leaving only the burnt stones to commemorate the family which had built and betrayed it.